by now, *Welcome to Scar Ridge* is as much horror as it is a western.

"Which, I believe, is the natural stage in the lifespan of the western genre: the location is isolated, desolate, and naturally hostile to life; the world is still untamed there, making it a place where the demonic, the supernatural, and monstrous people can thrive; none of the characters are who they seem, whether they're running from something, or they're chasing something. Indeed, the typical archetypes for the genre haven't been twisted, they've just been left to develop. And that development is horrific and, oftentimes, tragic. Which the reader will know before the characters do, in a dramatic irony that interlocks as much as the stories themselves do.

"In many ways, the horror western parallels the gothic horror.

"You don't need to like westerns, or be able to tell a horseshoe from a hee-haw, to enjoy what Johnathon Mast has written. Really, if you've read or watched any kind of fiction, you already have the basics. What Mast does is not allow you to shy away from the advanced western the basics are capable of developing into. It's not something you'll find in any dime store... if you could still find dime stores, that is."

~ Carl R. Jennings, author of *Just About Anyone*

PRAISE FOR
WELCOME TO SCAR RIDGE

"This ain't your granddaddy's western. In fact, if Rod Serling himself scooped up the Ponderosa, Dodge City, and Walnut Grove then plopped them right smack dab in the middle of *The Twilight Zone*, it still wouldn't hold a candle to the wild weirdness of Scar Ridge. Jonathon Mast will keep you turning the page with this hellish collection of bandits and lawmen, cowboys and Indians, soiled doves and the salt-of-the-earth dealing with high strangeness in a Weird West all his own. Welcome to your next can't-put-down read, *Welcome to Scar Ridge*."

~ Jason J. McCuiston,
author of *The Brotherhood of Secret Darkness and Other Cults, Cabals, and Conspiracies*

"From the moment you read the opening few lines in the first story of this collection, you are made aware that Scar Ridge is not your average Old West town. The first and last stories actually serve as bookends of sorts for what is an excellent collection of short stories.

"I enjoyed how certain characters and locations appear throughout the book, with Danzig's General Store and the twin saloons almost feeling like characters within the intertwined tales.

"Honestly, there is not a bad story in this collection, and I am hard pressed to choose one as my favorite. There is a little something for every horror fan in this collection, which is a quick, fun read.

"5 out of 5 stars."

~ John Watson, Horror Book R&R

"As much as this sounds like what someone would expect me to say about a horror book, I'll say it. I would not suggest reading this book right before you go to sleep. Or do, if that's what you like. Strange dreams await!

"As I read through each of the nine interconnected stories, I wondered how they would be tied together at the end. Each vignette brought another weird, peculiar, and unsettling way Scar Ridge affects its residents. Strange plants appearing and disappearing, things going missing, and the dead? Well, they have their own issues. And why is there a train station if no rails are going in and out of town?

"*Welcome to Scar Ridge* by Jonathon Mast is the perfect length if you'd like just a little bit of something scary and bizarre to give you a break between other reads."

~ Rachel J. Pierson,
contributing author of *#EduMatch: Snapshot in Education*

"There was a time when western novels had the reading public's attention tied up on the railroad tracks, as the three-ten express barreled down the line. People devoured western novels with such a speed that publishers couldn't hope to slake the appetite. As such, the quality slipped. This is where the term 'dime store novel; came from: formulaic westerns were written at speed (and produced on a budget) just so something new could be put on the shelves.

"Those days are past now; the western novel no longer holds the sway that it did. That isn't to say the western has gone the way of *The Penny-Farthing Owner's Manual* or the *Guide to Dodo Bird Husbandry*. When I was a kid, [redacted] years ago, the major bookstores still dedicated entire shelves for westerns. Today, they're in their own little tiny grouping—the most popular and well-known names have circled the wagons—but their legacy lives, dispersed through the tropes of so many other books: the outlaw with a heart of gold; the soiled dove with a troubled past; the man running from something; and the lone protector, doing what they know to be right against all odds, just to name a few.

"What Johnathon Mast is doing with *Welcome to Scar Ridge* is not so much a Trojan Horse of the western novel, but a dust-and-blood-caked boot knocking down the door.

"The titular Scar Ridge is the center point, in one form or another, for the collection of short stories. The small desert town is foreboding, hostile, unsettling, and oftentimes downright eerie. That is, when it's not an outright Hell. If you haven't guessed

WELCOME TO SCAR RIDGE

BY
JONATHON MAST

From

Dark Owl Publishing, LLC

Arizona

ALSO FROM
DARK OWL PUBLISHING

Collections

The Dark Walk Forward
John S. McFarland

*The Last Star Warden
Volumes I and II*
Jason J. McCuiston

*The Phantom World:
A Last Star Warden Adventure*
Jason J. McCuiston
Available only on Kindle

*The Last Star Warden:
The Crimson Star Saga
Episodes*
Jason J. McCuiston
Available only on Kindle

*No Lesser Angels, No Greater
Devils*
Laura J. Campbell

*The Tension of a Coming
Storm*
Adrian Ludens

The Nightmare Cycle
Lawrence Dagstine

The Art of Ghost Writing
Alistair Rey

*The Brotherhood of Secret
Darkness and Other Cults,
Cabals, and Conspiracies*
Jason J. McCuiston

Bad Dreams and Reflections
Trevor Kennedy

Anthologies

A Celebration of Storytelling

*Something Wicked This Way
Rides*

Novels

The Black Garden
John S. McFarland

The Mother of Centuries
The sequel to *The Black
Garden*
John S. McFarland

The Keeper of Tales
Jonathon Mast

Just About Anyone
Carl R. Jennings

The Malakiad
Gustavo Bondoni

Carnivore Keepers
Kevin M. Folliard

The Wicked Twisted Road
D.S. Hamilton

For Young Readers
Annette: A Big, Hairy Mom
John S. McFarland
The sequel is coming 2024!

Grayson North, Frost-Keeper of the Windy City
Kevin M. Folliard

Shivers, Scares, and Goosebumps
Vonnie Winslow Crist
The sequel is coming 2024!

Buy the books for Kindle and in paperback
www.darkowlpublishing.com

This one is Andrea's fault. Blame her.
I'm pretty okay with it, though.

TABLE OF CONTENTS

A DRINK WITH THE DEVIL

1.

Full moon.

Carter hated full moons. That's when the weird stuff came out.

He just wanted to get home. He'd followed all the trails back to Scar Ridge; through the Superstition Mountains, keeping to Darren's Trail until he sighted the turnoff, through several dry creeks, over a few spurs of the mountains.

The saguaro loomed over Carter, staring as he rode past. Jacob, his horse, didn't seem to mind. Nothing much bothered him unless someone was shooting at them. That tended to bother both of them.

Right now, though, it was them, the moon, and the saguaro. Jacob's hooves thudded into the rocky ground. It had been a long ride. One last rocky outcropping to turn past and he'd be in sight. His heart ached.

Home. Weird as it was, as much of a pain the people were, it was home.

Carter turned his gaze down on the valley. The moon shone down on what should have been Main Street. There should have been Danzig's General Store and the saloons and the schoolhouse and all the other buildings. Especially the little house just past Candide, the happy saloon. This late everyone should have been in bed except maybe Danzig counting his change and Major in the saloon, and maybe a certain woman waiting up for him. But Scar Ridge wasn't so small that the buildings went away at night.

There were no buildings. No sign of human habitation. Instead, saguaro stood in a circle, like some sort of witch's hoop. They pointed up to the sky, their arms all turned to the center of the circle. Inside, bare shale and the sand of the desert floor shone white in the moon's light, like fresh-fallen snow.

Carter rested a hand on his pistol.

Weird stuff. Always the weird stuff.

Jacob stopped at the edge of the circle. He refused to move forward, flicking his ears and not moving a hoof.

Now Carter unholstered his pistol. His breath was too loud in the silence of the night. Where were the buildings? Where were the people?

Where was Bess?

Even if something happened and everyone had to run, there would still be buildings. And Bess would leave some sort of message for him. She'd want him to find her.

He dismounted, his eyes scanning the cold-lit valley. More saguaro. Sagebrush. Nothing moved. He stepped to the edge of the circle and crouched, reaching out his hand to touch the ground within. The sand of the desert could shine white, but this seemed to glow.

What he felt wasn't the grit of sand. It was soft as flower petals.

No. It *was* flower petals.

"You're late."

His pistol aimed at the voice faster than he could think. It may have fired a few times, too, but no one would be able to tell by the person leaning against a saguaro like it was the corner of the post office. He wore black. Black denim pants, black boots, black shirt, black hat. The white light of the moon seemed to vanish in his clothing.

His skin, though, was the bright white of the sand inside the circle. He took a drag off a cigarette as he straightened. "You have arrived. I have awaited you. You owe me rent."

"Rent?"

He threw the cigarette down and ground it into the sand—flower petals—whatever—inside the circle. "Rent. I am the Landowner. Did you think you could live in my valley without paying for it?" He shook his head. "I supplied everything here for you. Now it's time to pay up."

Carter didn't move his pistol from him. "Buddy, I don't know what you're talking about. I'm just trying to get home."

"I presume you reside in Scar Ridge?"

"Yeah."

"It is no longer here, as you can see. I have come to call and take what is mine. Everyone has been loaded onto the train except you."

"No trains come to Scar Ridge. Ain't no rails."

"And yet you have a train station."

"Yeah. Never made no sense to me."

The Landowner shrugged. "Just another thing I supplied for you in my valley. But I am running late. My train has places to be. Of course, I've been able to amuse myself while waiting with some of the residents in the meantime." Dark eyes flicked to Carter. "But I desire that everyone pays what they owe. Everyone who resides here. I want them all to belong to me."

2.

Carter kept his pistol pointed at the Landowner. "You've got to the count of now to tell me what the hell you're talking about."

The man's smile sprouted on his face like some sort of weed. "Your mayor was quite the betting man. He liked high stakes. Blackjack was his game of choice. He tried to win the town back from me." He shrugged. "It didn't work quite so well."

Carter glanced around, never taking his eyes off the Landowner for more than a second. "No. No way. I've heard of some fellows that won businesses in betting games, but that don't make the business disappear."

The Landowner shrugged again. "I suppose when you're human it works that way. Now, would you like your town back? I do so enjoy games, you see, and I can be a fair sport. If you'd like, we can make a little wager. If you win, you get your town back, and even all the people in it. But if I win, well, you come along as obediently as Jarvis's cattle." That grin grew wider.

"Why don't I just shoot you and take the town back?"

He laughed. The sucker laughed. And then that smile again. "Well played, sir. Perhaps you should. Perhaps it would be proper for you to seek revenge and slay me with your, ahem, mighty weapon. But perhaps you might consider how you shot me three times, and all you have done is damage my wardrobe." He pointed to three holes in his shirt. "Surely you wounded this body, but I am not knit together as you are. So, yes, sir, you may shoot me all you wish. And then we may make our wagers, if you are willing. Or you may ride from here, never to see your beautiful town that you think you have sacrificed so much for. Oh yes, Carter, I can scent the blood on your soul, like my mistress's pies in the evening. But come, sir, a wager?"

He knew Carter's name. This bastard knew his name. And he stole the town. But Carter's eyes landed on the holes in the man's shirt. Carter'd met plenty of men with bullet holes in their clothes, but those men tended to wear shirts they'd stripped from the dead. He spied black holes in the flesh beneath.

This was no man, whatever he was.

But this is where Scar Ridge was supposed to be. This was his home. This is where Bess waited for him. And all that was left was a circle of saguaro.

Hell. He'd already lost his soul long ago. What's one more game with the devil?

Bess was worth it.

Carter shook his head. He told himself to get his head in the game. He couldn't think about her. Just focus, just like when he was on a job. Just do the job and get paid, like anything else.

Just this time, he'd be getting paid with his home.

And if he lost, he'd be just as dead as in any other job.

"A wager, you say."

"Indeed, sir." The Landowner tilted his head. "Choose your game. I find that it adds excitement when I don't choose."

Carter rolled the thought around his head a moment. "I'm only good at two things: Killing and drinking. And you already showed me I can't kill you. That leaves drinking."

That slow smile again. And he nodded. "A fine competition to select. Do you have a drink of choice? I'm afraid my usual favorite might prove strong for your simple palate."

Carter raised an eyebrow. Now, he'd been in cities where they served smooth sake and good port, but they'd never much appealed to him. Give him a good beer or a good whiskey and he was happy. But challenge him, say that something was too strong for him? That rubbed him the wrong way. "And what do you usually drink?"

He shrugged. "I imbibe deeply of fermented nightmares. A finely aged concoction of losing one's teeth and centipede legs simply makes me giddy. But, alas, such distilled spirits cannot exist on this plane."

Carter ran his tongue over his chompers. He hated those nightmares. "All right. Whiskey then. Straight up. Whoever can hold their liquor best wins."

The man in black gave a slight nod. "Agreed."

Carter held out his hand.

The Landowner stared at it, his nose wrinkling just a little. "Why do you humans insist on corporeal touch to seal agreements made in good faith?"

"I don't agree to nothing with a man that don't shake on it. Can't trust a man like that."

"And can I trust a man like you, Carter?" His eyes shifted from the offered hand and up to his eyes. "A man who shoots his prey in the back? Your scent sings treason. I can smell symphonies of it. The brave hunter, returning to his town with resources to share with his woman. What would she think if she knew who you were, I wonder?"

"I protect my own. That's all that matters. Now shake on it, or I ride out of here. Maybe shoot you a few more times before I go."

He sighed. "I must complete my collection." And he put his hand in Carter's. His skin was soft like a banker's.

Carter never liked bankers. They were always thinking about numbers instead of people.

They shook.

3.

"Now. I suppose I must conjure some of your whiskey." The Landowner raised one of his banker-hands and indicated the space behind Carter. He turned to look.

There Candide stood, right where it ought to be. Oil lamp light flickered through the wax-paper windows.

His eyes raked the landscape around it. No other buildings. Danzig's was still missing. No houses. Not even one where a woman should be waiting for him. Just a circle of saguaro. Just a full moon.

Just a saloon.

"Come, come. I do have other obligations to attend to." The man in black led the way through the swinging door.

Carter took a deep breath. Jacob still stood outside the saguaro circle. Who could blame the wisdom of a good horse?

But he'd shaken on it. Even to a banker he'd keep his word.

How much could a devil drink? Probably more than a man. Bu at least he could still shoot him, even if he couldn't kill him. Maybe it would make him feel better when he lost.

Wait. He could still shoot the Landowner.

Carter smiled.

He marched into the saloon. And then he stopped.

Before the bar stood Major. He wore his red flannel shirt like always, no matter how hot it got. He had his stupid mustache, that huge handlebar thing that made him look like he was trying too hard. His shirt lay open, and instead of nipples he had two taps. And as Carter took him in, his eyes fell on the man's boots. Well, where his boots should be. He didn't have any feet. His legs grew together somewhere halfway down his shins until what rooted into the ground was a saguaro.

"Carter?" His glazed eyes passed over him. "Are you home? I thought there were just girls here. Girls." He smiled. "My girls."

The man in black strode behind the bar and plucked up a mug, returning to the bartender. "I desire a repast." He turned on one of the taps sticking out of Major's chest.

Thick blood oozed out of him. He groaned, at first as if a girl were pleasuring him, and then as if he were a saguaro bending in a dust storm. His knees knit together until he was more saguaro below the waist than man.

"I win, everyone goes back to normal?" Carter asked.

The devil turned back, taking a deep glug of blood. He sighed. "Should you be the victor of our wager, you may do what you wish with your people. The town shall come to you, what is the term, 'as-is?' Oh, with one condition. It'll be your town. You'll have to protect it. And I'll still be the Landowner. Everyone will still owe me, one way or another." He gulped from the mug again. "Ah. So much better than any of your so-called liquor." He licked his lips.

Carter eyed Major. "Is everyone like this?"

"Oh, no. Your banker has scorpion tails instead of fingers. He is currently trying to make love to his wife, who of course greatly fears him. Meanwhile she is slowly melting, making it rather difficult for her to run away. Her legs keep bending in awkward ways. It is quite a comical turn, if I do say so myself. And there is a woman who wears a blue dress that is slowly becoming younger and younger. She knows she is growing younger. She knows she is forgetting her life, minute by minute, hour by hour. Oh, I do believe she has forgotten you now. She knows she has lost something of great value but can't fathom what it could be. I wonder how much younger she will be before we complete our wager?"

Carter growled, pacing back to the bar. He grabbed out two handfuls of shot glasses and a bottle of whiskey, slamming them on the bar. "Come here. I need to make this right."

"If you say so. Or perhaps I will win." The Landowner smiled. "I believe I will hold my drink better than you will."

Carter set his pistol on the bar and poured the first shots. "Drink."

They slammed back those first drinks. The heat coated Carter's throat. Major never had good whiskey, but Carter was used to bad stuff.

The man in black grimaced. "How barbaric. Pour another."

A second.

"Poor Johan. Your banker has caught his wife, but his scorpion fingers have pushed right through her skin. Her scream sounds like she's eaten too much pudding, but it's just her vocal chords melting. Delightful."

A third.

Carter felt his brain slide ever so slightly inside his skull. It was that good feeling of not caring. The man in black blinked at him.

Major groaned again. "The girls, Carter. The girls." Needles grew from his upper lip instead of hair.

The man held up his fourth shot. "Oh, look at that. I guess she's not a woman anymore. Just a girl. Pity. I guess she could still be waiting for you, but she'd have to call you her father now."

Carter growled and slammed back his fourth drink.

The Landowner slapped his back. "She's crying. Trying to write down everything she remembers, but it's flowing past her so fast. Faster than a man's blood pours out of him when you shoot him."

They took their fifth shots. The room spun ever so slightly.

The Landowner raised an eyebrow. "Care to call it quits? It would be terrible if you blacked out before I could have any fun with you." He paused. "Oh, it's so hard to hold a pencil in fingers that are that little, isn't it? Poor girl. Have you ever seen someone age themselves back before birth? It's a horrid sight. Very slippery."

Carter slammed back a sixth. The Landowner shrugged and answered in kind.

Major held his hands up as if they were saguaro arms. The walls of the saloon writhed with spiders. The moon was too bright.

A seventh. Black danced at the edges of Carter's vision.

"I do believe you fight a losing battle, my friend. I have won this wager."

Carter held up an eighth shot in his left hand. "Like hell. Let's make this better. You win, you don't just get me, but I'll hunt down whoever else you might want." The words sloshed in his mouth and in his mind. He had to get this right. "I'm a good hunter. You know it."

"I could use another agent for when I am… indisposed." the man in black considered.

Carter pressed on. "But I win? Everyone goes back to normal. Just like that. From before you got here."

He nodded. "For your boldness, and your hopelessness, I will accept this addition to our wager."

Carter plucked up his pistol and shot the man in black right in the gut.

He rolled his eyes. "You cannot harm me."

"Maybe not, but I just won."

The Landowner raised an eyebrow. "I am not inebriated in the least."

"Maybe not, but you ain't holding your liquor." Carter pointed at the hole in his stomach.

Whiskey flowed from it.

The Landowner's eyes narrowed. "Clever." He looked up at the moon, now just above the horizon. "And my time here draws to a close. You have won yourself a town. I shall return next year to make good the debts of the people here. One year."

The ground seemed to pitch up around Carter. One too many drinks. "Sure, buddy. Just make everything right again."

"Done."

And with that, the man in black vanished, and Carter passed out.

ALL SAINTS

1.

Mark rode toward the town from the East.

Scar Ridge. It looked like a scar, sure enough. Some old thing that spoke of pain, that the people here survived just out of spite. Two main roads ran through the town in a T shape, colliding at the train station. No rails came into town, though, and no rails left.

Still had a train station.

Mark squinted. Messed-up town, sure, but it meant no one was likely to find him here. Not if there wasn't a train that ran through, and no mines producing anything of note, and no wagon trains passing by. There was no reason for the town to be here at all, and yet, there it was in front of him, a line of buildings erected on the dust of the desert floor.

He pulled the letter from his belt again.

Please send a parson. We need a holy man for All Saints Chapel in Scar Ridge. Pay and housing included. Must be holy man.

He huffed a laugh. Holy. Sure. He could fake that. The corpse that he'd picked the letter from sure wasn't going to help anyone here.

He sighed and urged the horse on. An old church stood on this side of town. That's probably where he should go first. Big graveyard next to it, too. Stones angled out of the ground in all sorts of shapes. Some nice statues. Looked like there might be more dead people in Scar Ridge than living ones. Well, he'd been among the rotting before. This would just be a little more formal, that's all.

The horse nickered.

"Shut up," he rasped. Stupid horse.

They came closer to the church. Its steeple pointed to the heavens, a dark cross at its pinnacle. There was probably some sort of bell in that tower. The building itself was an old white thing, probably hadn't been painted this century. The whole place looked like it might fall over if there was a good gust of wind. The graveyard stretched behind it, and beyond that was a low building. A house? Maybe.

He rode around to the front of the church. A man with a wide-brimmed hat whitewashed that side of the building, or at least as high as he could reach.

As Mark came in sight of him, the man crouched and spun, pointing a rifle at him. "Stranger," the man said.

Mark nodded from the saddle. He didn't make any fast moves. Stupid. Should have been ready, not looking around like an idiot. Well, he'd had guns pointed at him plenty of times before. What's one more? Keeping his eyes on the gun, he asked, "You called for a preacher?"

"A parson," the man answered. The rifle didn't move. "We need a holy man, not just someone who says pretty things."

"I don't say much that's pretty, but I got your invitation." Mark pulled the letter out and waved it toward the man.

"You might be who we're looking for, then. I was just working on the church, trying to get it a little better looking. The chapel's seen better days." The rifle still didn't relax. "You got a name, stranger?"

"Mark Dies."

"Not a great name for a parson."

"I never thought it was a good name, either." And that much was the truth. Not a good name for much of anything, especially considering the kinds of people he usually spent time with. "It's what my dad gave me, so that's what I kept."

"Johan Schmidt. I'm the mayor here. I wrote that letter."

"That's a real formal name. This a formal church?" Mark shrugged, doing his best to ignore the gun. "I ain't much for formality."

"Then you might do well here, long as you preach on Sunday

and bury people when they need it."

"Oh, I think I can handle that." Sounded simple, really. Just one more thing to fake.

"We'll see, Parson. We'll see."

2.

"There always that many spiders in the rafters?" Mark craned his neck, studying the inside of the chapel.

"You prefer bats?" Johan shook his head. He still carried his rifle, but at least he wasn't aiming it at Mark anymore. "You from some big city church that don't believe in spiders?"

"Oh, I believe in spiders. All sorts of things, really. Just seems like there's an awful lot."

"People don't spend much time here when we don't have a parson. No reason to clean. I've been keeping up the property best I can, but I don't have as much time as I'd like."

"Oh?"

Johan nodded. "I'm also the banker of the town. Decided that today would be a good day to whitewash the chapel, though. Good thing. I wouldn't want you wandering around town without someone to introduce you around. Might not go well, unless you were wearing a collar. You don't believe in collars, either?"

"I ain't Catholic, Johan. Just a good Christian is all."

"Mm."

"There a lot of Catholics here?"

"No sir. Just people. Germans, mostly. Got a few English folks. All sorts, I suppose. I just take care of their money, when they have it. Take deeds for the properties. Take care of the building here." He paused. "Try to do a better job of that since my wife... Well. That was about half a year back."

Mark sauntered around the building. "What happened?"

"A difficult night for everyone in the town. Things are mostly back to normal now, though. Most of us just try to keep on moving."

Mark made his way up to the pulpit in the center of the front of the room. It was a huge, light wood edifice. He imagined everyone's eyes on him. It was Thursday, so he'd have a few days to get used to the idea. "What kind of services you used to?"

"Mostly whatever the parson gives. We'll show up. Fire? Brimstone? Something smart? Something simple? Don't matter to us none. Give us something, and bury the dead."

"You always bring your rifle into church?"

"Only when I feel the need to."

Mark turned toward Johan. "You feel the need to?"

The man narrowed his eyes and didn't answer.

He could shoot Johan. He was sure he was faster than the banker with the whitewash stains. It'd be a first for him, shooting someone in a church, but it would just be one more thing on his list of sins. He really didn't want to add to that today, though. This could be a good place to lie low.

"So this here's the chapel," Johan said, without acknowledging the tension in the room. "Parsonage's on the other side of the graveyard. Place is yours for as long as you're laboring here. You didn't ride in with much. Good. A man learns better if he travels lean. Can I show you around town?"

3.

"Welcome to town." Johan strolled down Main Street.

Mark glanced around. The sun pounded down at them. Not many people moved around at this hot hour. Buildings lined the road. A few horses were tied to rails in front of the buildings, but even the horses seemed pretty scarce at the moment. Everything seemed a lot older than it probably should. No fresh paint anywhere. Wind-aged wood on just about every surface.

He frowned. "Where'd you all find the wood for the buildings? Ain't no forests around."

Johan shrugged. "We make do. That's the blacksmith's. Just the blacksmith. It doesn't have another name. He's worth quite a bit to the community. And these two businesses. I wouldn't expect a parson to frequent them, but you should know about them, all the same. That's Candide. That's Sallow. They're our two bars. Candide's where people go to feel good. Sallow's where they go to feel bad."

Mark glanced at the two bars. Both were two stories. Music jangled out of both. "Which one you drink at?"

"I drink at home. It's cheaper. This here's Danzig's. It's our general store. Danzig's another man who's worth a lot to the community. You should probably get to know him. And there's Butterbee's. He's our butcher. Good meat there. He takes care of the ranchers."

Mark sighed. Not really a lot happing on this tour, was there? It was a town. Just another town. A few bars. Little odd on how Johan described them, but he'd seen odder. There was that place back in Kaston where the owner dressed in a pink dress and prided himself on his drooping mustache. If he could drink at a place like that, he could drink at these. He wondered if the girls were at Candide or Sallow. Or both.

Well, maybe. Johan thought a parson shouldn't drink. That could be a problem. Mark drank, and that wasn't going to change.

"That's the sheriff's office. Sheriff Carter. He's not worth much, but he mostly keeps the peace in town. Only been at it about six months."

"Same time your wife died?"

Johan didn't seem to hear the question. "We haven't had a shooting in a little while. I don't worry about thieves at the bank, and that's a mite better than a lot of banks out here."

"You said the sheriff's not worth much?" Mark asked.

"That's what I said. That's most of the town."

And they'd made it up Main Street. Johan hadn't mentioned a number of places they'd passed. Mark thought he spied a barber, maybe a schoolhouse, some other places he should probably visit. Before them loomed a narrow building.

The German gestured. "And this here's our train station."

"Why's there a train station if there's no train tracks?"

Johan shrugged. "Sometimes it's best here to just accept things. Scar Ridge isn't exactly normal, Parson. Most of the strangeness leaves you alone as long as you leave it alone. It helps if you're holy, though. So I wouldn't worry if I was you."

"Right."

"Anything you're going to need tonight?"

"Just some grub."

"We'll head to Danzig's and get you kitted out. Butterbee's, too. You know how to cook, right?"

"I can make sure I don't starve."

Johan nodded. "Good. We don't want you starving. You'll have to start burying people soon enough."

4.

They got some bacon from the butcher and some flour and coffee from the general store. Johan paid for it all with barely a grunt. Maybe this would work out well.

Mark tried winking at the girl that ran the counter, but she didn't seem to pay any attention. Well, he could probably change that. Girls loved forbidden love, and if a parson wasn't forbidden, who was?

Probably a Catholic. He couldn't fake being a priest, though. Too many bells and whistles.

Wait. Parsons could get married, couldn't they? Maybe he wouldn't be that forbidden. Did that mean all the old ladies would try to get him to marry their girls? He couldn't decide if that would be good for him or not.

Well, if it meant he could convince the girls to spend time with him alone, maybe it would be good.

He and Johan headed back to the chapel just outside of town. The horse grazed on the dry grass in front of All Saints. Mark loaded the supplies onto the animal. "Well, Johan, where am I staying?"

"The parsonage. It's over there." He nodded across the grave-yard. "I'm sure you want to get settled. Keep the graveyard taken care of. It's one of your primary duties, taking care of the dead. It's what gives you worth. That and Sunday preaching, of course."

Mark nodded. "Of course."

"I'll let you go then. I'll stay here, work on the chapel for a bit. No one'll bother you much unless we need you. See you Sunday, then." He finally set down his rifle and picked up a brush, re-turning to his whitewashing.

Should he say something? He elected to take the horse's reins and start moving across the graveyard.

The stones were laid in straight rows in the dust. Each bore a name. Most of the stones were fairly plain. Every once in a while, a stone angel pointed to the sky or to the earth.

The horse nickered.

"Come on." He pulled at the reins again. Not too hard. He didn't need to hurt the horse. He should probably name the thing if he was going to keep this one for a bit. Probably wouldn't be good for the parson to steal horses. Not as long as he was going to be a parson, anyway.

No dates on any of the stones. Was that normal? He'd put enough people into the ground, but he never stayed around for the funerals. He shrugged. Maybe it was just another way the town was a little odd.

The low house stood right on the edge of the graveyard, not even five paces between the last stone and the house's walls. It was the same wind-blasted, sun-bleached wood as most of the town. No stable, of course, but there was a little fenced area behind the building. Good enough. He took his saddle off the horse and rubbed it down. He had to make sure it was ready to ride if he had to run quick. He'd know Sunday, probably, if the town was going to accept him.

He let the horse loose in the fenced-in area. Plenty of dry grass there. He'd have to go back into town and get some oats or something, but it should be fine for now. He turned to examine the building.

The parsonage had a low roof. He ducked his head as he stepped through a creaky door. Glassless windows let in the bright light. A smooth wood floor greeted his boots. The entire thing was one room. A narrow bed stood in the corner. Washbasin and pitcher on a stand. Nothing fancy, but he'd been in worse.

His boots sounded loud on the floorboards. The walls groaned in a breeze. That would be a problem. He wouldn't be able to hear anyone riding up, and he wouldn't be able to sneak, either. He didn't know much about carpentry, but maybe he could figure something out.

At least he wasn't in town. He glanced out the windows. He could see all the approaches. The graveyard stretched out two directions from the house. He examined the stones. Someone could sneak up easy that way. He'd have to memorize what the stones looked like so he'd know their silhouettes. He'd have a few days, though, from what Johan said.

All he had to worry about was Sundays and burying people. Simple.

5.

Mark swung the door open. "What?" he spat.

Johan stood before him, hat in hand.

He was glad he kept his pistol hidden behind the door. That would probably ruin his cover.

"It's Anna, Parson. Anna Penwich. She was found dead last night. Lived in town for years. Probably longer than the town's been here. We need a funeral."

Mark forced his eyes open. "Someone's dead."

"Anna, Parson."

"And you needed to wake me up before dawn?" His mouth felt like a grave. Probably shouldn't have broken into his whiskey last night.

"The dead don't wait, Parson."

"They wait fine. Don't bother no one."

Johan's bushy eyebrows drew together. "Parson, this is your job. Take care of the dead. If you can't do that, this isn't the place for you."

He took a deep breath. "Right. Fine. I don't wake up easy none. Give me a minute to freshen up, and I'll meet you at the church."

The German stood in the doorway a moment longer, then nodded and put his hat back on. He lumbered off.

What time was it? Must be just before dawn. He hated waking this early. Nighttime was better for everything. He swung the door shut and leaned against it, rubbing his eyes. It was hard enough being human this early, much less pastorly. Johan was lucky he hadn't gotten shot.

He threw on his cleanest set of clothes and stumbled across the graveyard to the church. How was this supposed to work? Was there someone to play organ? Piano? Guitar? Maybe they expected him to do it. He should have thought of that before. Maybe this wouldn't be so easy after all. The letter hadn't mentioned music, and neither had Johan.

The front doors of the chapel stood open, leading into the

large inner room. Still lots of spider webs in the rafters. Wooden benches led to the front. A couple lamps had been lit.

He really should have grabbed some coffee before coming over here. Maybe pissed, too. Yeah. Parsons pissing during preaching wouldn't be good.

He giggled at that thought. Preaching parsons pissing.

Up at the front was a table. What was that called? An altar. Yeah. An altar. Nothing fancy. Wooden cross on it. A couple candles.

And a book.

Well, he was a parson. Of course there was going to be a book. Probably a good one, too. He stepped up to the table—no, altar—and glanced at it.

No. This wasn't the good book. Pretty sure, anyway. It was a service book. Already open to the funeral page. That was helpful. He glanced through it. Not long. Good thing. He probably wouldn't be able to read much without coffee or pissing. A couple pages was all it was. He could spit that out, even with the thees and thous.

"You're the new parson?"

He startled and spun, barely keeping himself from drawing his pistol. A man in a dark suit, bowler hat, and a mustache stood in the chapel's doorway. He removed his hat. "Clive Staples, Parson. We'll be seeing each other a lot, as I'm the only undertaker and you're the only parson."

"We'll be seeing each other a lot?"

"There is an awful lot of death in Scar Ridge, Parson. And that keeps people like you and me awful busy."

6.

"If you'll help me bring her in, I'd be gratified." Clive motioned out the door.

Mark set the service book back on the table—no, altar. He really needed to work on this language thing. He followed Clive out the doors. A low wagon pulled by two horses waited outside. A plain wooden box lay in the wagon.

"This Annie?" he asked.

Clive raised a dark eyebrow. "Anna. This is Anna Penwich.

You better get the name right for the funeral or you'll have the town angry at you already. I'd really rather not have them run another parson out of town."

"They ran the last out?"

The undertaker shrugged. "Wasn't his fault. People can get awful particular. You know how it goes with religious folk."

"I take it you're not religious?"

He huffed a laugh. "When you work with the dead as much as I do, you either get very religious or you reject it all. Here. You take her head. I'll take her feet."

"Which is which?"

"Doesn't matter much, does it?" Clive climbed into the wagon and hefted the far end of the box.

Mark grunted as he lifted his end. "I thought dead people were lighter than this."

"You'd be surprised."

The two of them strained but eventually brought the coffin to the front of the chapel. They set it across some of the benches, and then rearranged them so the coffin lay across the front of the room. Clive reached to open the lid.

Mark stopped him. "Wait. Shouldn't you not? Flies and stuff?"

The undertaker shook his head. "She died last night. No maggots yet. There's a reason we want her buried quick, though. Nothing worse than having to look at someone while maggots wriggle through their hair. She's safe for now." He propped the lid open.

Inside lay a woman that Mark guessed was in her fifties. Long gray hair with a few dark streaks framed a wrinkled face. She wore a plain, faded blue dress with a white flower embroidered on her left shoulder. Her hands were folded over her stomach. She had delicate, clean hands.

"Who was she?" Mark asked.

"You remember her name?"

He wrinkled his nose. "Anna."

"You thought about that too long."

He sighed. "Yeah. So I never had to do a funeral for someone I never met before."

"Anna Penwich. Her husband ran herd for Gerhard Hanover years ago. Died in one of the stampedes. After she rented out her home to ranch hands when they needed a place in town. Good cook from what I understand."

"Thanks. Those are things I can talk about."

Clive chuckled. "Good. Mention one or two things, and everyone will tear up and call her a good woman. Then we'll take her out to the graveyard and bury her good."

Mark nodded. "Sure."

The undertaker stuck a hand into his suit jacket and retrieved a flask. He took a swig and offered it to Mark.

"You sure we're allowed to do that in here?"

Clive shrugged. "I take it you're not religious?"

Mark accepted the flask and took a deep pull. "Tastes like shit."

"Sure does."

He downed another few gulps. "Clive, I think you and I are going to be able to work well together. Mind watching the chapel so I can find a place to take a piss?"

7.

Mark stumbled through the funeral. The words weren't normal for his mouth. He usually only said words like "God" or "Jesus" in ways that the good people here would probably frown on.

Actually, they probably wouldn't have any problem with that language, unless it was coming from someone they thought was holy. Well, Mark wasn't holy, that much was sure. But they didn't have to know that.

Maybe Clive could know that. He stood in the back of the chapel, arms crossed, a smirk on his face.

Mark embellished a little, adding how Anna was a good woman who served God and the community. A few little old ladies who sat on the front benches wept. The men who sat next to them kept their arms crossed and their eyes on the front wall. Thankfully someone came up to the half-mangled piano in the front of the church when Mark suggested they sing "Amazing Grace." It was a woman. Another person Mark would want to get to know, he guessed.

While they sang, the women in the front of the chapel wept

louder.

When Mark said the final "Amen," six men stood and approached the casket. Clive stepped forward, lowered the lid, and nodded. They looked up at Mark.

He was supposed to do something. What were they waiting for? There wasn't anything in the book. The funeral was done, wasn't it?

Clive gestured toward the door.

Oh! Mark clutched the service book and walked out the back of the church. The pallbearers followed, carrying Anna's corpse. The congregation filed out after. Mark spotted a few men leaning on shovels in the graveyard. He headed over that way. The pallbearers set the coffin down. He found the place in the service book and stumbled over Psalm 23. Too many thees and thous. No one seemed to notice.

They lowered the casket into the ground. Everyone there tossed in a handful of dirt. Then everyone dispersed back to the town.

Clive stayed behind and supervised the burial. By then the sun beat down on them. He wiped sweat off his forehead. "You did good, Parson."

Mark shrugged.

"Be ready to do it again."

8.

Saturday morning. Mark lay on the mattress as the house creaked and groaned around him. It was almost dawn.

He should probably start thinking about whatever he was going to bullshit from the pulpit tomorrow. It would have to sound holy enough for everyone. It shouldn't be that hard, but he should really find a Bible. There'd be one in the chapel, right? Hell knew he didn't own one.

A heavy knock sounded. He suppressed a grumble as he shuffled to the door and swung it open.

Johan waited for him, hat in hand. "Parson. It's Niles Pemberton. Passed away last night. I'll head over to the chapel and open it up."

"Another funeral?" His breath smelled like the grave.

Probably worse. Clive had been kind enough to share more of whatever he kept in that flask.

"Course, Parson. What do you expect? But you did fine yesterday. Bury the dead. That's the idea."

"I haven't even met anyone here yet, besides you and Clive."

"You'll meet everyone tomorrow. Today, another funeral." Johan trudged away.

Two funerals in two days. The old lady—what was her name?—whoever it was he'd buried yesterday hadn't been shot. It wasn't some sort of sickness. A town this big shouldn't have that many deaths, should it?

He sighed and slipped on the same clothes from yesterday. Maybe he'd have to request that the chapel provide something nicer for him to wear. He should get a tie, maybe. He'd look good in a tie, right? Maybe he'd be welcome at some of the better card tables when he moved on if he had a tie.

He trudged across the graveyard. Took maybe five minutes to get across. By the time he made it to the church, Clive was waiting for him. Another wooden box sat in his wagon. "Told you we'd be seeing plenty of each other."

Mark grunted as he moved to help lift the coffin into the church. "Who's this?"

"Niles Pemberton. Didn't Johan tell you? One of his workers at the bank. Guess he caught ill."

He pulled his hands away from the casket. "Sick?"

"I wouldn't worry none. Probably pneumonia or plague or something."

Mark pressed his lips together. Probably wouldn't be good for the parson to shoot the undertaker. After a moment he sighed and hefted his side of the box. Once it was placed at the front of the chapel, Clive offered his flask.

"What is this anyway?"

"Best you didn't know," he answered, taking the drink back after Mark had his swallow. "That way if someone smells it on your breath, you claim innocence. That trick only works once, though."

The people filed in. The old women wept. The men were stoic. Mark read from the book, said a few extra words, led the people out to the graveyard. The box went into the hole.

Everyone went home. He and Clive shared a few more swallows from the flask.

Johan trudged over to them. He eyed Clive and turned to Mark. "Parson."

"Johan."

"Might be you ought to wake a little earlier. I don't like having to knock to find you. Maybe out east they sleep in, but we work here."

"I'll keep that in mind."

"And if you're going to drink, do it after dark. We need a holy man to bury us."

9.

Sunday. Mark forced himself up before dawn. The horse nickered as he stepped out of the house. "Yeah. I still need to name you. I know." He trudged across the graveyard. His breath clouded the air before him. He wrapped his arms around himself.

Clive didn't wait outside the chapel this morning. Well, that was good. Maybe a normal day for once.

Right. Because he knew anything about the Bible. Because he could fake being a parson. The last few days, people had been clouded up with grief. They weren't paying attention to him. Not really. This morning, though? They'd be able to smell him out.

He really needed to get another set of clothes, too. Maybe get one of the women to wash what clothes he had.

Yeah. He really had to talk to some of the women.

He opened the doors and entered the dark building. His boots banged against the floorboards. Shadows flickered in the rafters.

Maybe it was spiders that was killing people. Some of them were venomous, after all. If all the buildings in Scar Ridge were like this one, people could be dealing with a lot of critters that weren't too fond of humans. He should probably head into town, anyway. Johan'd gotten him plenty to live on for the first few days, but a man needed more than bacon and coffee. And whatever Clive had in that flask of his.

He lit the lamps. Took a look at the service book. Looked like there were words for a Sunday. That was good. He still couldn't find a Bible anywhere. Did they expect him to have his own? What fool would carry a Bible around? Or did they think he had the whole thing memorized?

He flipped through the service book and found some pages filled with what he thought might be Bible verses. Anything he could make something up about? He squinted.

"Psalm 5:6. Thou shalt destroy them that speak leasing: the LORD will abhor the bloody and deceitful man."

Sure. God could abhor all he wanted. Lots of people abhorred Mark, but he was still here. He could talk about bloody and deceitful men, though. Probably as fine a verse as any to start with.

About an hour after dawn, people started filing into the church. A few rushed forward to shake the new parson's hand. They wore suits and dresses. The men took off their hats. The women kept theirs on. More than a few of the women raised their eyebrows, taking in Mark's clothes.

"I've not had the time to clean up yet," he apologized each time. "Haven't found someone that takes in clothes."

Every once in a while, the woman's eyes would widen. "Yes. I may be able to help you with that, Parson."

"I'd be much obliged. Should I come by later?"

Well. As long as he could get through this morning, between the women and Clive's drink, maybe this wouldn't be a bad place to lay low after all.

The same man found his way to the piano. He waved Mark over. "Got any songs you want to use today, Parson?"

"I think you know best what people like."

"That I do." He started thumping away some dreary thing about blood and clouds, but as soon as he did, the gathered people joined in. They seemed to know just what to sing. Mark had no idea what the song was, except there wasn't anything in it he was interested in.

He stumbled through the service. Bullshitted through the talk in the middle, which he took some pride in. Stood in the back to shake hands as people filed out.

Johan nodded. "Parson." The man had clean, clean hands.

The pianist grinned. "Parson." He had some callouses on his

fingertips, but nowhere else.

"Oh, Parson!" One of the women who might take in his clothes blushed. Her hands were very, very clean.

"Parson. I'm so sorry." An old woman offered a muddy hand for him to shake. Her faded blue dress was dusty. Even the white flower embroidered on her shoulder seemed to wilt a little. "I was happy to hear you speak, though. I'll be sure to stay away from deceitful men!"

"Be sure you do." Mark nodded and brushed his hand off on his pants leg.

The next person in line filed in front of him. She invited him to her home for Sunday lunch. It would be an honor. He accepted, of course. She and her husband had two boys and four daughters, all of them various shades of marrying age. Mark wasn't much interested in the marrying, but the girls caught his eye. The second oldest, in particular, had a shape that even her shapeless dress couldn't hide.

They had him over to a house near the town, a short walk away. He was served chicken pie and vegetables. Good food. Better than just bacon and coffee, to be sure, but the drinks needed to be stronger. Oh, well.

They invited him to sing at their table. He stumbled through a few songs. Most of the tunes he knew probably would make the girls laugh, but he was sure the parents wouldn't appreciate them.

Eventually he finally got to head out. He wasn't even given thirty seconds alone with any of the girls, which made it difficult to enjoy his time with the family. Hopefully he behaved well enough that he'd get welcomed back for food, though. Oh, what was the family's name?

Eh. Didn't matter none, really.

He passed through the graveyard on his way home. The thing seemed smaller on the way to church this morning. Maybe he was just tired. He paused next to a headstone to take a deep breath.

And then he frowned.

He'd been paying attention to some of the women folk, not all of them. Many of them were older than his tastes. But there was that one with the dirty hands. Most of the women had very,

very clean hands. They came in clean dresses. But there was that one woman. She had a familiar face, but a good chunk of the town had come out to the funerals.

There was something about that face, though. What was it? He had seen it at one of the funerals, he was certain.

Anna. It was Anna.

It was the woman he'd buried.

10.

Mark needed a drink. Oh, he needed one badly. None left of what he'd brought, of course, and he had no idea where Clive lived. Should he go into town? It was early evening. No reason he shouldn't go in.

Except he was supposed to be respectable. He was supposed to be the parson.

Screw it. A man needed a drink once in a while, and getting your hand shaken by a dead woman was one of those times that would make saints drink. Hell knew, he was no saint.

The horse didn't want to take the saddle. He swore at it. Anyone else hearing that would know he wasn't a parson, but the horse didn't seem to care one way or the other. It just wanted to keep cropping the dry grass. Now he really wished he'd named it something.

It took some doing, but he finally settled in the saddle and set off for town. The sun was just touching the horizon.

No way it had been the same woman. Maybe she had some sister or something. He didn't remember anyone who looked like the dead woman sitting in the chapel that day, but really, would he have noticed? It would have been just another lady crying into a handkerchief.

Except the woman this morning had the same dress, and it was all dirty. And her hands, too, like she'd just climbed out of a grave.

But she'd been nice enough in line, right? If someone came back from the grave, they were supposed to be mean. They'd be out for revenge or something, not sitting in church like all the nice ladies were supposed to.

The horse plodded onto Scar Ridge's Main Street. Windows

lit up in yellow squares of light. Not a lot of people out. A few other horses heading here or there. A few people on foot.

"Parson?"

The voice startled Mark. He glanced around until he spotted a figure in a dress near one of the buildings. She held a bag. He squinted. "Yeah?"

"It's me. Marta Evans. You had lunch with my family today."

Marta. Which one was that? He urged the horse closer. Ah. That one. The one who had the nice figure. Looking into her face now, he noted a spray of freckles.

Well, how do you distract yourself from a dead woman? Find a living one. Maybe even better than finding a drink. Maybe.

He forced his face to relax. Maybe even grin a little. "Marta. I'm sorry. I'm meeting so many people, and I don't recognize everyone right off. I really should have recognized you, though." He winked. "Some people are too pretty to forget."

Even as he let his mouth run on, the back of his head still crawled all over the idea that maybe there was a dead woman walking around.

Nope. Didn't matter. Girl now. Dead woman hopefully never. Ignore the old lady. She didn't matter none. She wasn't here anyway. The girl here was. Marta. The dress didn't exactly help her figure, but imagine if it was lying next to his bed back at the parsonage. Much better.

The girl's cheeks reddened. "Well, Parson, I just saw you riding in. Mama needed me to borrow some flour." She hefted the bag in her arms. "She's setting out some dough overnight, you know, but we ran out."

"Well, you're doing a fine thing for your mama. I was wondering, since we've run into each other like this, maybe you could do a fine thing for me?"

Maybe it was the angle of the sun, but Mark was pretty sure her blush deepened. "Well, maybe."

"I don't have much in the way of clothes, and what I got, maybe you noticed, it ain't very respectable. Maybe you could hop up here, ride home with me, and take some of my clothes to clean them up? I'd be much obliged."

Marta glanced away, toward her home. "It wouldn't be proper for me to be unaccompanied in the home of a man."

"I suppose so. I'll see if I can find someone else to help me out." He moved to turn the horse away.

"Oh, Mama would want me to be neighborly, I'm sure. And that's what the good book says, don't it? To love your neighbor." She sounded hopeful.

"It does say that." He was pretty sure it did. He'd heard as much somewhere. He extended a hand. "Come on up. Ride out with me, and I'll take you home again. Won't take any time at all."

11.

The sky turned the purple of a hanged man's neck as they rode through the graveyard. Marta rode sidesaddle behind Mark. Her shoulder leaned against him though, and that was a nice feeling. The horse stopped in front of the parsonage. Mark helped the girl down, and then dismounted himself. "Home," he gestured.

Marta watched the graveyard, though. "Parson Welles laid Grandpa down just a few years ago."

"Out there?"

"Where else?" She glanced up at him. "Makes a girl feel a little nervous, being near all those stones."

Oh, he could handle this. "Well, it's a good thing you've got me here to protect you." He stretched an arm around her shoulders and hugged her close. "Nothing bad can happen to you as long as I'm here."

"You're a holy man," she said.

"Course I am. And you're here to help me. So come on in and rest a mite while I gather up my clothes." He swung open the door.

Its creak echoed against the gravestones. He tried not to think of one of those graves that might be empty. No, no. It couldn't be empty. It was just his imagination is all. He'd seen men go a little sideways when they were under stress, and there was some stress here, with him pretending to be someone clean. It was fine.

The girl ducked her head and stepped into the parsonage. She looked around. "I ain't never been in here, Parson. It's so bare."

"A man don't need much." He closed the door after himself. "And I don't need much either. Just some clothes, some bacon, some coffee."

"And God's Word," she added.

"Of course. That too." He grinned. "And it helps having a good woman to take care of a man."

"Of course." She looked up at him with a lopsided grin. "And I could take care of you real good. Mama's taught me how to cook and sew."

"That's not what I need right now."

"What do you need, Parson?"

His mouth came down hard on hers.

Not long after Marta sauntered from the parsonage. "That's enough for now, Parson. I expect you to talk to my pa if you'd like something more." She shifted the dress at her shoulder.

Mark tried not to grumble as he followed. She wouldn't take the dress off. What use was a girl like that if she didn't take her dress off?

Well. Maybe it would be a challenge. And maybe she'd be worth it, as long as her pa didn't chase him down after. He should probably take better care of the horse if he was going to have to ride out of town in a hurry, though.

He took her home. She took his clothes and the flour her mama had sent her for. She winked at him. "Thanks, Parson. I'll be happy to come back out soon."

"I expect so, Marta."

He rode home alone. No drink, no empty dress next to his bed, but at least he'd had a little bit of a distraction. He didn't have to think about Anna, the dead woman, coming to church that morning.

Nope. He didn't have to think about her at all. There was no empty grave. There couldn't be. That's just not how things worked. Buried people stayed buried.

And hopefully he didn't have to bury anyone tomorrow.

12.

Nope. He had to bury someone tomorrow. Course he did. The

knock came before dawn, as the other ones had before. Johan waited. "Parson."

"Johan."

"August Bartz. Shot up last night at the Sallow. You know how it goes."

"I really don't. Not been there yet. Was he a good man?"

"Who cares?" Johan stepped away. "You bury him, parson. It's your job."

Clive waited by the chapel, a cigarette hanging from his mouth. "We meet again."

"Yeah. Took me forever to get here. That graveyard seems bigger every time I cross it."

He shrugged. "Well, we are putting new bodies in almost every day. Take your end."

Mark grunted as he lifted. "Why are they always so heavy?"

Clive didn't answer.

"Could've used your flask yesterday. What'll it cost for me to get a jar of whatever it is?"

The undertaker raised an eyebrow. "More than they pay you."

They set the casket at the front of the church. Clive wiped off his forehead. "I really wish I had an apprentice."

"You hiring?"

"Hell no. They don't pay me enough." He offered the flask.

Mark accepted.

"You said you could've used it yesterday?"

"Never mind."

"Saw you talking to the Evans girl last night. Watch out with her. She likes teasing men. Knows they like what she's got."

"Oh?"

He took the flask back. "Buried two men lately because of her. Well, because of her pa, technically. Sheriff Carter wasn't happy, but the judge let the man go with a few nights in the jail." He shrugged. "This guy, though, he had it coming."

"Oh?"

"You won't have too many people crying over him, is what I'm saying. August was a bastard. Cheated at cards, treated the women at Candide like they belonged to him, and stole more than a few head of cattle in his time." Clive took a deep draw from the flask. "But he's still gotta be buried. And you're the man to do it."

"Hm." They stood in silence for a while, looking down at the casket.

"I think I'm pretty proud of this one, though." Clive gestured to the box.

"Yeah. It's good wood. Where do you find wood around here? Ain't no trees."

"Not the wood. The body. I figured, no one like August, so if I messed up his face, it wouldn't bother anyone. Been trying to get a little better at making people look peaceful-like, you know? Here." Clive popped the casket open. "Take a look."

A pale man with a bushy dark mustache and bushy dark eyebrows lay within. He wore a cheap gray suit with a shiny green bolo tie. Clive looked up at Mark expectantly. "Well?"

"Well what?"

"He look natural?"

"Sure. Natural as a dead person can look."

"Exactly! This man lost all his blood. Well, not all of it, but a lot of it. Was a real mess. But you'd never guess. That's artistry a man can be proud of. Next time we get a few people shot here, I'll bet you won't even be able to tell after I get done with them. Make them look real good." He reached in and brushed some stray debris from the dead man's suit. "Not every undertaker can do that, you know."

"Haven't been to many funerals."

"Really?"

"Give me your flask again."

Clive handed it over.

Soon enough people started showing up for the funeral. Just a few crying women this time, along with a few somber men. Mark read from the service book. The words were getting way too familiar in his mouth. He led the procession from the chapel.

On the way out, he almost tripped and fell right on his face.

A woman in a dirty pale blue dress stood in the back of the church, singing.

Anna.

13.

Screw this. Screw all of it. Mark buried the dead man and marched right into town. Two bars, right? One for happy, one for sad? Fine. Sallow it was. He took a seat at the bar and accepted the rotgut the bartender gave him. And then he downed more. And then another. Felt good to finally get something real in his belly, not just bacon and coffee. He really would love more of Clive's drink, but he'd take the beer.

He glared around the room. It was a narrow place with a packed earth floor. No lamps were lit yet. No need. Sunlight filtered through a dirty narrow window behind the bar. The bartender was a thin man with a patchy beard. His clothes were dirtier than Mark's were when he'd arrived. The cloth he used to wipe out the mugs was even dirtier.

Well. At least he fit in at one place in this town.

A few other people drank at the bar. No one talked. No one said a word. When they wanted more, they raised a finger. The bartender limped over to them, handed over a mug, took their change.

Simple. Quiet. Exactly what Mark wanted right now. Perfect.

So. Dead woman. No one else seemed bothered by her. Just one more woman in the congregation. A woman with dirty hands.

Was her grave empty? He had no idea which grave was hers. The place was big enough, he'd probably have to search for hours to find the stone with her name on it. If it had her name on it. A bunch of them didn't have any names. Maybe Clive would know.

But of course, the only time he saw Clive was when there was a funeral, and there were already enough of those. It was supposed to be so simple to hide out here. Parsons only worked an hour a week, he thought. Well, in most places, they did. Not Scar Ridge, though. Of course, he chose to lay low at a place where people kept dying.

He raised his finger for another beer. As the bartender came over, Mark asked, "People always dying here?"

"Most people do eventually." He handed the mug over.

"No. Every day. Someone else dies. It ain't normal. I've been enough places. Parsons don't bury a person a day. Pretty sure, anyway."

The bartender shrugged.

One of the other patrons staggered from the bar and rushed outside. The door muffled the sound of vomiting.

Yep. This really was the kind of place Mark was used to. Perfect for him, really.

Except he was a parson.

Someone came in and sat on the stool next to Mark. Flies buzzed. Something smelled a little rotten, like meat that had just turned. Mark huffed. Maybe it was the butcher.

"You gonna bury me right next time?"

Mark glanced over at his neighbor. And then he fell off his stool. Beer splashed over him.

August. The man he'd just buried. He sat on his stool. Flies swirled. Dirt clung to his pants, his hands, his face. The man turned and glared at Mark. "I asked you a question."

"Um...?" He couldn't breathe. How was this possible? Dead people don't get up. Especially not after they'd been shot up. Mark had shot enough people to know.

"You gonna bury me right next time? Only a saint can lay a sinner to rest."

Was it cold in here? His teeth chattered. "I ain't no saint."

"Oh, we figured that out." August tossed back his beer. "We figured that out real easy. And now look at me. Your fault, Parson. You clean yourself up so you can lay me to rest. I don't wanna rot anymore than I gotta, hear me? It's your job to lay the dead to rest. You signed up for the job. You better perform it."

14.

To hell with this. Mark was getting out of town. He burst from Sallow and sprinted down the street toward the church.

This is what God did to people who pretended to be a parson, huh? Set them up in a crazy town where dead people come back and yell at you? He wasn't trying to hurt anyone! Not here, at least. He just wanted to rest up for a little bit before going back to his old life! He wasn't even planning to rob the bank before leaving!

He heaved for breath and stumbled against the wall of the church. His horse was just over there, at the parsonage.

Across the graveyard.

He'd only buried three people. One was that August person. He was at the bar, right? Still trying to drink away whatever it was that he was now. Maybe that would work. You could drink yourself dead. Could you drink yourself alive? He never even saw the face of the second person he'd buried. And the first was that woman who liked singing at the church.

But the graveyard. He'd hidden in graveyards plenty of times before, but that was before dead people started coming out of them. He'd seen August and Anna both buried. They were dead. They weren't breathing. Clive would know that!

Clive. Did he know about this? Did he know that dead people came back?

It was that undertaker. He'd been drinking whatever was in that flask. It was good, but what if it made him see things? He knew there were plenty of drugs out there that messed with a man's senses. That had to be it. Dead people don't get up. They don't get angry that they're still alive. After all, if they were alive again, they should be happy. Yeah. It was just whatever Clive had been giving him. That's all.

Mark nodded. Of course that's all it was. That's all it had to be. As long as he didn't drink any more of Clive's flask, he wouldn't see any more dead people. Nice. Simple. Done.

His heart finally slowed down. He could think again. Maybe he'd had one beer too many. Probably not. That couldn't be the problem. He could hold his drink better than that.

Well, whether it was the drink or anything else, he was done in Scar Ridge. He'd had a few days, but it was time to move on. Too bad about Marta. He'd liked to have gotten that dress all the way off her. No. No, not worth it. If her pa already killed two men, he'd come after Mark, too. And there were plenty of other women around.

Right. So just get to the parsonage, saddle up, and ride out. Whatever dead person showed up at the church tomorrow would have to find someone else to bury him.

And to get to the parsonage, he had to cross the graveyard.

It was just a graveyard. Sunset now. Still plenty of light. It's not like anyone could sneak up on him. He narrowed his eyes. No one moving out there, alive or dead. Right.

He took his first step away from the church, and then the second.

Nothing moved.

He frowned. He should be able to see the parsonage from here, shouldn't he? Sure, it was on the other side of the graveyard, but it wasn't that far away. Couldn't be. No. He was just confused, was all. The house was just over there, and the horse was behind the house. Just a few minutes he'd be there, and a few minutes past that he'd be on his way farther west.

He passed the first row of headstones. These ones were old, judging by the wear on the rock. No names chiseled into them. He didn't think the town was old enough to have stones like that, but what did he know?

He knew that dead people don't really get up from their graves. Otherwise there'd be phantoms aplenty after him.

Mark kept his eyes on the horizon. The parsonage should be in view anytime now. The second row of headstones passed, and then the third. And then the fourth.

Where was the house? How big was this graveyard?

He glanced down. It was just the desert floor around him. Stones. Sand. Packed earth. Not much to hold a body down if they really wanted to come up for a visit.

He shook his head. That wasn't a good way to think. Not now. The dead stay dead. They weren't going to rise up and get him. This wasn't one of those stories that hands told around the fire. No reason to be nervous. None at all. It was just time to move on.

He walked for a few more minutes. Still no house out there, and the sun sank lower and lower. He looked behind. The church had vanished into the gathering gloom. Just endless rows of stones marking the final resting places of the dead.

And it was their final resting place.

He spat. No threats here. He was just turned around. All he had to do was keep walking. He'd get to the house eventually. He just got confused sometimes. He turned to head back to the parsonage.

He tripped over a headstone and fell on his face into the dirt.

Mark growled and punched the ground. He scrambled to his feet and glared at the offending rock. "Really? That's the best you got?"

He pulled down the front of his pants and pissed on the stone. "Yeah? Take that! You're dead. You can't do nothing to me!"

His voice echoed along the rows.

No one answered.

"That's right!" He tried pulling himself back into his pants and almost fell over. He chuckled. That would have been awkward. Probably painful. He finally succeeded in putting himself back together and resumed his voyage among the dead.

The sun vanished. A half-moon rose and shed a pale, dim light. Mark kept walking. He swung his head, searching for any sign of a house, of a church, of anything besides endless rows of stones. He stopped to piss on another stone. The stars turned overhead.

There had to be an end to the graveyard. He must have gotten turned around. Maybe those beers were stronger than he expected. He'd never been one to get lost, but that had to be the only answer. Of course he was lost. It wasn't that the graveyard had swallowed him. It's not like it could punish him for pissing or pretending to be a parson. Everyone pissed. It was human.

But what if he was trapped here? What if the dead really did come up again? What if August found him? If he shot a dead man, would he die again?

Mark spun. "Who's there?"

No one answered.

That's because no one was there. He flicked himself in the temple. Course there wasn't anything there. Who would be mad enough to be walking around a graveyard in the middle of the night?

Something like the sound of shifting sand slithered into his ears. He spun. His legs got tangled and he fell. He scrambled back to his feet, eyes everywhere, looking everywhere.

Nothing moved.

Should he run? Would it do anything?

There. A shadow in the distance, bigger than any of the stones. He broke into a sprint. More than once he fell. What did they put in the drinks in that bar? His heart thundered. If anything was chasing him, he didn't know.

He kept his eyes on the shadow. What was it?

Eventually it resolved into a house. His house.

Safety.

He stumbled to a stop and put his hands on his knees. He was just turned around. Everything was fine. He'd go in, get his stuff, mount up, and move on. Simple as that.

He straightened to finish his walk home. The chuckle died on his lips.

Outside the house, a shadow waited for him.

15.

Mark could go to the house, or he could go back to the graveyard.

He could face whatever the shadow was, or he could face whatever moved under the ground among the graves.

He growled to himself. There wasn't anything behind him. It was just his drunken imagination. That's all it could be. No threats there.

But the shadow. That could be a threat. Maybe it was whatever he thought was August. Or maybe it was Johan. Maybe there was another death. Maybe it was someone from the last town he'd hit. Maybe it was Marta's pa, even though he hadn't done anything a pa should be angry at. Mostly. She wouldn't let him.

A lot of maybes.

He took a deep breath. He wasn't going back to the graveyard. Not this time. No way. That meant he was going on. He was going to see whatever that shadow was. If he was lucky, maybe it was the devil himself.

As he came closer, the shadow resolved. Thin shoulders. Delicate neck. Not a man, then. He sighed. Marta? Maybe she'd snuck out in the night so they could have some fun. Even though he wanted to run, he'd take that kind of fun. He desperately needed to blow off some steam. He started thinking about what it would be like to peel that dress off her, the color of her bare skin in the moonlight. Yes. That is exactly what he needed.

And then he stopped short. The shadow moved toward him. It wasn't Marta.

It was Anna.

The light bleached her dress, but he could still see the floral pattern and the embroidered flower on her shoulder. It was definitely that old woman. She reached toward him with shaking hands. "Parson, something's gone wrong. I go home, but they don't let me in. I thought it was a miracle, but it's not, is it?"

He croaked.

"Parson. I need you to bury me again. It didn't take, Parson. What did I do? Why aren't I good enough? I just want to go home. Just lay me down, please. I need a holy man like you to set me to sleep."

He stumbled backward. He fell on his ass. He stared up at her.

"Parson? What's wrong?"

"You're dead!"

"I know. And I need your help. Please. I need a holy man to lay me down."

"I ain't holy."

"I hope you are. No one gets out of Scar Ridge unless they're holy. Please help me."

16.

The ground crunched under his boots. He didn't even take the time to get the horse. He couldn't.

The dead woman. She was really there. The woman he'd buried was back.

The moon shone down on him. He dashed as fast as his rubber legs could take him. His breath burned in his lungs.

Away. That's all that mattered now. He'd run, and when the sun came up, he'd figure out where he was. And if he died of exposure out in the desert, at least he'd be away from there. At least he wouldn't be in that mad place.

A sob escaped his lips.

No. No, he'd be fine. He was getting away. He turned, trying to get his bearings. It was just a flat expanse. No hills. No mountains. No buildings. No trees. Just nothing nothing nothing.

That was fine. As long as there was nothing around him, he

couldn't be near town. The dead wouldn't find him out here. And if they did, he'd see them coming. It'd be fine. He'd be fine. Or he'd be dead, and he wouldn't have to put up with Scar Ridge. Never again.

Eventually the sun rose. Still a plain expanse. Not even cactus. Not even pebbles. Just sand and sand and sand.

He was thirsty. He should have brought a flask. He'd take water now. Anything.

The sun beat down on him. Just an endless flat place.

No one gets out of Scar Ridge unless they're holy. That's what she'd said. But what did she know? She was dead. Dead people couldn't know anything.

Except maybe she knew.

No. He'd just keep walking. Eventually he'd find something. He had to.

The sun sank. His feet must have been bleeding. He didn't dare take off his boots. His tongue swelled up.

Still nothing.

Nothing nothing nothing.

Maybe the graveyard was better.

No. No, this was better. There wasn't anything here.

No one gets out of Scar Ridge unless they're holy.

And he wasn't holy. Not by a long shot. He thought about Joan. Had she given birth yet? Maybe. He didn't intend on ever finding out. What about Abel? His body had probably been found by now. The sheriff would know it must have been him. Oh, and all the whores. That probably meant he really wasn't holy.

And that meant he couldn't get out?

Screw that. He'd get out.

He drew his pistol and fired.

17.

He startled awake.

A dream. It had all been a dream. He chuckled. Of course it was a dream. Madness like that didn't exist in real life. No way.

Mark sat up. Or he tried to. His head thunked against a wood panel.

No.

He pushed with all his might. His muscles strained. Finally, the panel moved aside. Loose earth poured into the narrow space. He fought against it. He dug. He pushed up. Up! The soil tore at his fingernails. He heaved for breath.

Finally, he reached open air. He flopped to the ground next to a gray stone slab.

Anna stood over him. "Only saints get out."

JARVIS'S WIFE

1.

Mathilde squinted. "It's near?"

The man sitting on the seat of the covered wagon grunted.

"That's yes?"

He grunted again.

She didn't yell at him, though she wanted to. It was more than he'd communicated during most of the grueling voyage from out east. One should never punish what is a step forward, and the grunt was indeed a step forward.

She just really wished it was more of a step forward.

She brought her head back into the interior of the wagon. The other women whispered to one another. A few worked threads into various designs. They all had that anxious look that Mathilde refused to wear.

Carrie looked up from where she sat on the wagon's floor. She was the youngest of them, only sixteen. "You find anything out?"

"Nothing more than normal." Mathilde composed herself and sat beside the younger woman. "I hope our husbands talk more than that man."

Carrie giggled. "I don't know. A silent man might be the best one to marry." Even as she said the words, though, Mathilde noticed how the woman's hands shook.

She took them in her own. "We've talked about this."

"Yeah. Doesn't mean I'm not nervous."

"Our contracts had very exact language. There are husbands waiting at the end of the trail. I'm to marry the ranch's owner, Jarvis. And each of you are to marry one of the hands. And they'll treat us all well, or I'll see them hanged." She grinned. "Or worse."

"You think my husband will care?"

"I've heard enough about the men out west. He won't know how experienced you are unless you tell him. He'll just want to have some fun."

"Oh, and that I can give him!" Carrie giggled again. Her hands continued to shake.

"We know the contracts," Annie said from Mathilde's other side. "We signed them. I don't think any of us are worried about the contracts. We're worried about the men. We've all got enough experience with men to know how dangerous they can be."

"Well." Mathilde huffed. "We're all apprehensive. We've had enough time to heal, though. I can't even tell you had that black eye when you signed."

Annie lifted her chin, a glare in her eyes.

"I wish I knew what kind of husband waited for me. What men waited for us. But at least we all get to start over. No one there will know what any of us were like out east. What lives we're leaving." Mathilde squeezed Carrie's hand. "We can be whoever we want to be. And I was serious about seeing someone hanged if they treat any of you badly."

"I really don't think the lawman will care about that," Annie muttered.

"Who said anything about a lawman?" Mathilde winked.

A half-smirk crossed Annie's face.

The wagon driver knocked on the wood of his seat. Mathilde raised her eyes. The driver motioned her up. With a grunt, she pushed herself onto her knees and scooted onto the seat. The driver waved toward the land.

"We *were* close," Mathilde whispered.

Cattle grazed a broad lawn. Small stands of trees dotted a dusty plain. Chickens clucked before a two-story house. It sat in the shade of the largest tree she could spot. Smaller buildings surrounded it, along with a large barn and a dormitory. Each of the buildings seemed devoid of paint. Each surface was wind-smoothed wood.

The girls poked their heads out behind Mathilde. Some gasped. Some nodded. Carrie trembled.

The oxen pulling the wagon plodded on. It seemed to take hours, but finally they pulled in front of the house. A broad covered porch wrapped around it. A man in a broad-brimmed hat and a thick mustache waited on the front stairs.

As the oxen pulled to a stop, the man stepped down to the ground and spat tobacco juice. "Well. Time to call the parson. We got some weddings to do."

2.

Mathilde walked with Jarvis, the man with the hat and the mustache. "How long until the parson gets here?" she asked.

"Parson Dies will get here when he gets here." His manner was matter of fact. He kept his eyes on the horizon of the ranch even as they walked.

"What kind of work do you do?"

"What do you think, woman? I ranch." The words might have been harsh, but his tone remained plain. "I ride out with the hands. We brand cattle. We drive them to market." He gestured. "But it's a lot of sky out there. A lot of land. It makes a man lonesome. Needs someone to keep him company that ain't another man or a cow, as pretty as some of them are."

"Cows are pretty?" She had no idea how to respond to that.

"Some of them. You look them in the eye, and you know they're thinking something. Don't rightly know what. Their mouths ain't made to form words. But some of them, some of them..." He didn't finish the thought.

She let the words linger in the air. The other women were being greeted by the hands, back by the wagon. Many of the hands grinned to see the ladies. Some laughter floated over the dry lawn to them.

"Your hands seem hospitable."

"Oh, they're good boys. I'll see to it they treat the women well. Won't hire a man that'll beat a woman. This world's hard enough. I won't put up with someone making it harder. That's one of the things I'll expect of you, woman. You'll spend more time with their wives than I will. You hear of anything untoward, report it to me. I'll see everything taken care of."

"Really?" Her voice was small.

"I'm a gentleman." Again, the tone was matter of fact.

"I've met gentlemen that'll beat a woman without thinking."

"That ain't no gentleman. No. If anything harms you here, it won't be me, and it won't be the hands. We take care of women here." He still didn't look at her when he talked, though.

"Why won't you look at me, Jarvis?"

His eyes remained on the horizon. "Sometimes a man doesn't want to get too attached. I told you I won't harm you. That don't mean there aren't other things out there. Dangerous things. I've been attached before, and it didn't turn out well."

"You said a man gets lonely. That sounds awful lonely."

"It is, woman."

"I have a name."

"I'm sure you do. Most things do. That cow there? Her name's Greta." He walked over to the cow and put a hand on her head. "She's a good cow, ain't she? Look at those eyes."

Mathilde did. She gasped. "She looks so sad."

"Well, maybe she sees something that makes her sad." His voice got real quiet.

Greta lowed.

"There, there. It'll be fine, I'm sure." He patted the cow on her shoulder and hugged her head. "Nothing bad's going to happen to you, either." His voice caught as he said it.

"I don't understand."

"Woman, we're in Scar Ridge territory. There are a lot of things we don't understand. But you're here now. You'll be my wife. We'll walk this road together until we can't anymore."

3.

Parson Dies rode in and slipped from his saddle. His clothes were far more worn than Mathilde would have expected of a minister. He looked like a hollow man. He stumbled over to Jarvis. "These the ladies you brought in?"

"I did, sir."

He looked at Mathilde. "You want to marry him?"

"I signed a contract back east to do it."

"Fine. Fine. Gather everyone up. Let's do this." His voice was rough, like he'd been drinking. Mathilde wasn't sure she wanted to be married by a man like that.

The parson stood on the steps in front of the house. Mathilde stood next to Jarvis. She reached to take his hand. He shook her off and simply stood beside her.

What was wrong with her? She knew she wasn't as good looking as some of the girls. Was that it? He'd rather have been marrying Carrie? Or had she said something wrong? Did he resent her for mentioning the contract in front of the parson? Maybe she had embarrassed him. Whatever the cause, it wasn't a good way to start a marriage, was it?

Behind them in a line, the hands took their places next to the girls. Seven more pairs of people. Not every hand was getting married that day. The others spread out across the lawn as witnesses.

The parson hefted a book. "Right. Dearly beloved, we've gathered here today to witness the union between this man and this woman."

Mathilde blinked. Was he just reading the words, not even bothering to change them so it fit what was going on? There was more than one man and one woman here. All the parson did, though, was read from the book. He didn't say anything extra. Nothing much about love. Just words from a book.

Finally, he said the amen. The hands behind them whooped and hollered. She turned to see a number of the girls receiving deep kisses. Carrie's new husband seemed particularly excited.

She looked up at Jarvis. His eyes still scanned the horizon.

"Aren't you going to kiss me?" she asked.

"Time enough for that tonight." He stepped away. As he moved through the crowd, several hands slapped him on the back. Someone took out a fiddle, and soon a dance had broken out. Some of the unmarried hands brought out food from the house's kitchen; beans and cornbread and slabs of beef. Soon enough, apple pies joined the feast.

Jarvis, though, went and stood by one of the cows. Greta? She didn't know how to tell cows apart. But what kind of man left his bride on the day of their wedding to pay attention to a cow?

What was wrong with her that her husband wouldn't even look at her?

Someone handed her a tin plate of food. She ate without thinking. Someone handed her a mug of beer. She drank without tasting. Someone with calloused fingers took her hand and spun her. She danced without feeling.

The sun dipped toward the horizon. The dances continued. Men handed women off to each other for turns with them, but most of the women ended up back with their husbands by the end of any song. Some of the hands belted out what tunes they knew. Some of the women joined in.

Carrie found her. Her hands weren't shaking. "I'm going to have so much fun tonight."

Mathilde pushed her numbness aside. "Looks like you're already having fun."

Her cheeks reddened. "I think Malcolm's going to be good to me. In a lot of ways."

"Good." She hugged the younger woman.

"Woman." An even voice called to her.

She turned. Jarvis hovered nearby. His gaze still floated above the crowd. "Come with me," he said.

She nodded. "Carrie, have a good night. I'll see you tomorrow."

"You have fun, too!" she hollered before turning back to her husband. He nuzzled into her neck and kissed her. She squeaked.

Jarvis walked through the crowd. Many of the hands shook his hand or slapped him on the back. He greeted each one by name. Those same hands tipped their hats to Mathilde. She nodded back to them. Her husband climbed the steps of the house. She followed. He opened the screen door and gestured her in.

4.

Jarvis climbed a grand staircase. Mathilde followed. He reached a dark wood door on the landing and opened it. He gestured her in. She obeyed. He followed. Her husband lit a match and used it to light an oil lamp near the door. He went around and lit three others in the corners of the room, revealing their bedroom.

Wood floor. Whitewashed walls. A plain bed. A dresser. A wardrobe. A plain room for a plain man.

He turned to her. His eyes remained on the wall. "Woman. This is our wedding night."

"Yes." What was she supposed to do? She knew how sex worked. She knew how to undress and do her wifely duty. She had signed the contract.

But how was she supposed to do that for a man who wouldn't even look at her?

He opened his mouth and closed it again.

"What have I done wrong?"

"Nothing, woman."

"You won't look at me. You won't use my name."

"No."

"Why not?"

He swallowed. "Well. I've lost many things. The hands need women. I brought them women. They're a loyal lot, though. Wouldn't take wives unless I had one myself."

"Do you not like women?"

He glanced down at her and flinched away. "No, woman. I like women. Like them a lot. Before I owned the ranch I liked them a bit too much, if you don't mind me being a mite blunt. I know some women don't appreciate that. If you'd prefer to sleep in another bed, knowing that, I wouldn't blame you one mite."

"So why don't you like me? What've you lost that's so important you won't even look at me?" She stepped closer to him. She smelled the dust of the field and the sweat of the day on him. "You're allowed to like me."

"I'm sure I am."

"My name is Mathilde."

"It's a good name."

"Do I have a good face?"

He finally turned his head down to look at her.

She gave a half-smile. "Is it at least as good as a cow's?"

He flinched away. "Woman. We're done for tonight."

"What did I do?" She was trying to make a joke. She was trying to help him relax. Why was she even doing that? She was the one who was supposed to be nervous. That's how it was supposed to work, right? The woman was nervous, and the man took the lead.

"Woman, I'll sleep in the bunkhouse tonight."

"You do that, the hands'll know you're not with your wife."

He stopped by the door, his hand on the knob.

"Come back. I'm not that bad. I promise." She stepped behind him. "You said you'd watch out for the women. You told me that you'd make sure nothing bad happened."

"Not what I said. Just said I'd make sure the men treated them right."

"All right. So treat me right. Look at me." She didn't even know why she wanted him to look at her. She didn't know him at all. Still, she desperately wanted his approval. "My name is Mathilde. I'm your wife."

He flinched again, but slowly turned toward her.

"Come to bed with me. If you're too nervous, that's all right. But come. Come to bed with me."

5.

Jarvis took a fresh shirt from his wardrobe. "You've certain duties."

Mathilde sat on the bed. She'd never fully undressed. "Yes?"

He slipped the shirt over his shoulders. "Take care of the house. Feed the chickens. Get me meals. I'll get my own coffee. Don't bother making any of that for me. Sometimes I'll eat with the hands. I'll let you know when I do. I'll let you know if we're fixing on guests, too. Mostly you'll have the run of the house, though."

"Is that all?"

"That's enough, woman." With that he fastened the last button. "And stay out of my office. It's the last door in the hallway up here. I'll join you for supper tonight." He shut the door after him as he left.

That was all.

She hadn't been expecting romance. Romance doesn't come from men who're willing to sign a contract to get a wife before ever meeting them. Still, shouldn't there be some sort of glow after the wedding? Shouldn't he have screwed her or some-thing? He said a man gets lonely. Lonely men screw. At least that's what she thought.

Instead, she sat in a bed, alone.

She eased herself off the mattress. At least it was comfier than any of the accommodations from the trip here. She told herself she should be happy. Jarvis could have been cruel. In-stead, he was just...

...well, what was he? She couldn't even really say.

Pale curtains covered the room's only window. She stepped up to them and pulled them aside. Jarvis strode the yard below, greeting the cattle. He put his hand on the heads of several of them. The hands did the same.

She frowned. Was that Carrie's husband? What had his name been? Malcolm. He was petting a cow's head, talking to it gentle. She couldn't make out the words from here through the glass, of course, but it was clear he was speaking with an affection she didn't expect from a hand.

She should probably get dressed. Fresh clothes might make her feel better. Of course, all the women had traveled light. The contract stipulated that they'd be provided with all they needed, including clothes. She wandered to the wardrobe and opened it.

Several dresses waited inside. She slipped one out and felt the fabric. It wasn't new, but certainly not worn. Good material. Simple pattern. Whoever had picked this out had done a good job. She'd seen plenty of shoddy dresses back east, and this wasn't shoddy. Mathilde slipped out of her traveling dress and tried on her find.

It fit perfectly.

She frowned. How was that possible? She didn't need to ad-just any of the drawstrings. It hugged her waist exactly right. It slipped over her hips as if it had been sewn for her. It even landed over her breasts just right. Not too tight, not too loose.

Nope. It was fine. It was just something strange. One more strange thing about the ranch. One more unexplained thing in Jarvis's house. At least it wasn't as unsettling as everyone being affectionate with random cows.

Cows with sad, sad eyes.

Of course all cows had sad eyes. Had she ever seen a happy cow? Well, she hadn't grown up on a ranch. Or anywhere near cows. But they weren't people. They didn't feel things. Cows weren't sad. They were just cows. That's all.

So. He'd be back for supper. She'd get a meal prepared for him. She knew how to cook. And maybe if she cooked something well enough, he'd look at her and not flinch.

6.

Jarvis sat at the head of the long table in the dining room. He nodded at the plate before him. "Fine. This is just fine."

Mathilde sat near him, gazing at his face. "Just fine?"

"What do you want, woman? I ain't much for poetry. The food's fine. The biscuits are softer than I'm used to, and the beef's softer. All good." He jabbed a potato quarter with his fork. "And the potato's got good seasoning. There. That good enough for you?"

The entire time he talked, he kept his eyes on the plate.

"I'm glad you like the food." She forced herself to keep her breathing even. "What about me?"

"I like you fine."

"You going to look at me?"

"You look fine."

She glanced down at the dress. "You pick this dress out yourself?"

"Hm? No. I don't know how to do those kinds of things." He waved a hand. "It's just a dress. Had it brought from town."

"How'd you know my size?"

"Hm?" He stabbed another potato chunk.

"It fits perfectly."

"Well. That's just luck, woman. Just luck. I don't know nothing about how anything fits a woman. You got all that extra fabric to cover all your pieces. I prefer denim for myself. Don't need nothing else." He glanced at her plate. "You need to be eating, too. Won't do anyone any good if you starve."

"I'm not hungry."

Jarvis shrugged and pulled her plate over. He stabbed a chunk of meat and stuffed it in his mouth. "I won't be letting any of this go to waste," he mumbled around the beef. "If you won't be eating, I expect you not to make as much. But you should be eating."

"It's hard to eat when the husband that paid for you won't even look at you."

He swallowed. "You're talking nonsense, woman."

"You want a wife or a maid?" she snapped.

Jarvis exhaled long and slow. He placed the fork next to his plate. He wiped his mouth with the red check napkin. He stared straight ahead. "I want a wife. I want a woman who'll keep me. I want a woman I can treat right."

"Well, treat me right," she spat. "Look at me."

"Told you why I don't."

"Right. You're too busy being all sad for yourself. Or something. I don't much care. You don't look at me. You just call me woman. I didn't expect romance. I didn't expect poetry. You don't get that from a contract. But I expected something. The hands were all excited for their women. How come you just look guilty?"

He stared straight ahead.

"You treat the cows better than you treat me."

"Cows don't leave." The chair rumbled as he stood.

"That's it? You're going to come home and eat? Is this what I got married for?"

"I don't claim to know what you got married for, woman. I know I didn't get married for accusations. Maybe I'm a fool to think a woman would do good for me. They ruined plenty other men."

"How many women did you ruin?"

She didn't see him move. The floor was under her hands. Her jaw burned.

"You will not say such things. Not here. Not to me," he breathed.

"Yes sir," she whispered.

"Now come upstairs. It's time for bed."

"I need to clean the dishes."

"I'll expect you in bed soon then." He stalked away.

Mathilde remained on the floor. She would not cry. No, she would not cry. This was her life now. This was her husband. He promised to treat her well. She should have known that this is what he meant. He'd treat her well as long as she knew exactly what he wanted and did just as he wished. Jarvis was a man just like any other.

She would not cry over such a man.

7.

Mathilde crossed the yard to the hands' houses. The cows watched her as she walked. She frowned at them. They turned back to the grass.

Jarvis was out riding the fences and making repairs, along with all the hands. Just the women for a day or two. She'd already taken care of the chickens. Not much else to do at the moment. Maybe she could visit the other women.

Carrie stepped out of one of the houses. A grin lit her face as she spotted Mathilde. The two embraced. "Look at you! Is that a new dress?"

She glanced down at herself. "It was in Jarvis's wardrobe. I don't know where he got it, but it fits fine."

"You look fine in it."

"Not like you!" Mathilde shook her head. "I'm surprised Jarvis didn't take you. You're practically glowing."

"Well, I'm eating a lot better than I ever have. My dress hardly fits anymore!"

"I'd lend you some of mine, but I don't think it would help!" Carrie winked.

"How's your husband?"

"Malcolm?" Her smile faded. "He's fine. He treats me fine. Doesn't hit me. And I showed him a good time on our wedding night. He didn't complain at all."

Mathilde waited a moment. "But?"

"I don't know. He was eager enough that night. And the next night. Every night, really." Her cheeks turned pink. "But when he looks at me, it's like he looks past me. Like he's not really paying attention. Or like he doesn't really see me at all. Like he's thinking about someone else when we're screwing."

Mathilde didn't answer.

"It's fine, I'm sure. It's just me. Never been with someone who might actually care about me, might actually take care of me. Just never been married before. What about you? What's it like living in the big house?"

She turned to take it in. "It's fine. Good food, like you said. And Jarvis. Well, he's fine."

"Don't give me that none."

"I'm sure I don't know what you're talking about."

Carrie clucked her tongue. "Really? I'm the one who's only sixteen. You're supposed to know more than me. That Jarvis of yours, he's not fine, is he?"

She didn't answer.

"We rode out here together. You're the only one who cared enough about me to talk to me. So I ain't leaving you now. Did he lay a hand on you?"

"Only once."

"You'd think the owner of a ranch could afford to treat his woman better."

"That's just it." Mathilde turned back to her friend. "I think he wants to. He talks about honor and all that. But he's scared of something, too. He says he doesn't want to risk losing me. I think, anyway. But I make him supper. He eats it fine. But at night." She shook her head. "We haven't been together yet."

It was Carrie's turn to frown. "Think he's deformed? Maybe he was in an accident. Terrible things can happen to a man. Or maybe he caught something!"

"I don't think that's it."

The cows looked up at them again, chewing their cuds.

"How's Malcolm treat the cows?"

Carrie's breath caught. "Strangest thing. He's got a favorite cow. That one, right there." She gestured to a brown cow that had a few white splotches on it. "Talks to it every day."

"The other hands do that, too?"

"Yeah. Every single one, I think."

"Something isn't right here, Carrie. But I don't know what."

"Want me to ask Malcolm when they get back tomorrow?"

She nodded. "Yeah. See if he'll talk. Jarvis isn't talking to me, that's for sure."

They spent the afternoon together. Carrie had to wash Malcolm's clothes. Mathilde helped her. She'd taken care of Jarvis's clothes the day before, so she didn't have to worry about it now. As the sun began to dip, they said their farewells.

Mathilde stepped into the ranch house. It was empty and silent. That's not the way the big house was supposed to be, was it? She'd think there'd be people bustling around, getting things done. Dogs underfoot. Fires crackling. Instead, quiet and darkness greeted her.

And a thunk. Something fell upstairs.

What could that be? Mathilde climbed the staircase and wandered to the left and down the hall. The floorboards creaked.

The first door stood open. Just an empty bedroom. Probably for guests. The second door, though. It was locked. Jarvis's office.

Something shifted inside.

No. It was fine. Just the house shifting. That's all it was.

A floorboard creaked again.

Outside, all the cows mooed.

8.

Two months later, her husband approached her. "You know how to use this?" Jarvis lifted a shotgun.

Mathilde raised her eyebrows. "Never had need to shoot one myself."

"I'll need to teach you, then. It's almost time to drive the herd to market. You and the women'll be here by yourselves for a month, maybe two." He kept his eyes over her right shoulder. Well, at least it was closer to her face. "You need to be able to shoot."

"Bandits?"

"If there's bandits, you get on one of the horses and ride for town. Sheriff Carter'll take care of them. Don't try to fight. Men do unspeakable things to women. I won't have that happen to my wife." His eyes flickered to her face for just a moment.

He looked at her. Mathilde felt a flutter in her chest.

"No, you won't use a shotgun on a bandit. You just run from them. But if there's coyotes, you'll need it then. Or anything else that's bigger out in the darkness."

"Bigger?"

"There are things in the hills. The hands talk about them sometimes. You'll be fine as long as you stay here or on the road to town. At least you should be. But it's best to make sure. So. Shotgun." He handed it to her.

His finger grazed her. Just a tiny touch.

The most he'd touched her since he hit her.

She couldn't figure if she should harden her heart or hope that they'd draw together. What kind of man was Jarvis? Even after all this time, she still hardly knew him.

The gun was lighter than she thought it'd be. She expected it to be heavy, like a bucket of water, but it wasn't nearly so much.

"Come out here. I'll take you someplace you can practice without hitting any of the herd." Jarvis stepped away. "Try not to shoot me in the back."

She carried it carefully, keeping her hand from the trigger. She'd never even touched a gun before. It hadn't been something she needed out east. That was another world, though. She followed him onto the porch and to the stairs.

She frowned.

"Something wrong?" He turned back to her.

"No. It's fine. Just... something about walking down the stairs here. I felt like I couldn't for a moment." She shook her head. "Silly. Sorry." She followed after him.

He watched her as she came down the steps.

"What's wrong?" She'd not seen that expression on his face before.

He forced a sad smile. "Woman, ain't nothing wrong. Can't a man appreciate his wife walking down some stairs?"

"That's the nicest thing you've ever said to me."

"I'll try and say some other nice things then." He turned and headed out beyond the hands' homes.

Her heart shouldn't be fluttering like that. Not over something so small. Not for this man. Or should it? He was a kind man. Most of the time. Oh, she hated this. She shouldn't feel so many things for just one person. It would be easier if she could just hate him or love him. She was jealous of Carrie, the way her husband treated her. Like someone he wanted. Like a person.

Mostly, at least.

Jarvis led her across a dry field to some fenceposts. Barbed wire spread across them. He stopped at one of the posts and looked back at her. "You coming, woman?"

"Course." She trotted to catch up, her hand still keeping well away from the trigger.

"Now," he said as she reached him. "This is a fine place to practice. Right out there. See that stump? Ain't good for nothing except target practice. And I made sure to get you the shotgun. Aiming ain't going to be hard with this. It won't kill much, not unless you're real close, but it'll hurt most things enough to keep them away. And the shot spreads out enough that all you have to do is point the right direction."

She nodded. This wasn't a surprise to her. She knew what a shotgun was.

"Now, easiest thing to do is lean on a post. Use it to steady you. This'll kick back strong enough. I don't want you falling over, hurting that rear end of yours."

"You don't care about my rear end."

"I do, woman. I care enough to give you a shotgun." He kept his eyes on the distant stump.

That was probably just as well. Carrie wasn't the only one putting on weight, but Mathilde had no idea how she could be gaining so much that she had to stuff herself into her dresses in the morning now. Maybe they were all eating better on the ranch.

"I want you to try to hit the target. Let's see how much we need to train you."

"Sure." She breathed out as she stepped up to the post and leaned on it. A gun. In her hands. She never thought about that when she signed the contract. She just wanted to get away from her folks. They were always so worried about doing what was right. She just wanted some freedom.

But a gun. It wasn't heavy. Not really. But it felt more real than anything else, somehow, like it could change everything forever.

No. All she was doing was shooting a stump. She could do that. It wasn't hurting someone. It was just in case. That's all.

"You gonna tell me anything else?" she asked.

"Pull the trigger when you're ready."

"Sure." She braced the shotgun against her shoulder. That's

what she was supposed to do, right? It felt awkward. She was probably doing something wrong. At least Jarvis wasn't laughing at her. Maybe he didn't know how to laugh, so it didn't matter anyway.

Her knuckle ached. She was probably holding the thing too hard. It wasn't a big deal. Just a shotgun. She could do this. Just shoot it. Just pull the trigger.

Thunder echoed. Her shoulder ached. She stumbled backward.

"Well, woman, looks like you've got good enough aim with that shotgun." Jarvis squinted toward the stump. "Hit it square on. Let's see if that was freak chance or innate skill. You got skill, that'll help a mite. Let me show you how to reload."

9.

"Malcolm stopped paying attention to me." Carrie sat under a tree, huffing, holding back tears.

"What happened?" Mathilde flexed her fingers. Since yesterday's lesson, her hands had been sore. She must have bruised something, too. All her nails had turned an ugly black.

The younger woman bit her knuckle. "We haven't made love in two weeks. He just spends more and more time out with that cow." She lifted her chin toward that same heifer. "And I'd think he'd pay more attention."

"Why?"

"Have you looked at me?" She brought her hands up to her chest. "I ain't never been this big before. Men usually like the bigger girls, right? He always liked me here before. But since I started putting on weight, these got even bigger. My back's getting sore. But he just doesn't care. He's even stopped talking to me."

And just when Jarvis was starting to talk to her.

Annie sauntered over to them and sat on the ground. "Mathilde. Carrie."

Mathilde frowned. "Annie. I ain't seen you in a mite. How're you doing?"

"Well, thank you." She practically glowed.

"Spit it out, girl," Carrie snapped.

"Oh, I have no idea what you're talking about." She rolled her eyes.

"You saw me crying up a storm and thought you'd come and rub my face in it," Carrie huffed.

"What's going on?" Mathilde asked.

Annie smirked. "Oh, I'm having a baby. Ain't had my time of the month since we got here. And look at me, already filling out some." She gestured to her belly and chest. That's not what caught Mathilde's eye, though.

"What happened to your nails?"

"Oh? I just banged them up is all." Annie glanced down at them. "They're just black."

"Have all the girls been putting on weight?"

Carrie shrugged. "Don't know. I've been pretty busy taking care of Malcolm."

Annie frowned, though. "Actually, yeah. Debbie was complaining that she was hardly fitting in her dresses anymore. I just figured she was being a pig."

Something huffed in Mathilde's ear. She flinched and looked up.

A cow loomed over her. Jarvis's cow.

The cow stared right into Mathilde's eyes. Those sad, sad eyes drilled into her.

"Anyone else bothered by the cows?"

"Yeah. Preston's got his own over yonder. Treats it as good as he treats me." Annie pushed herself to her feet.

"Anyone else bothered by them?" Mathilde asked.

"Yeah. But no one'll talk about them."

Mathilde stood, not moving her eyes from the cow. Her back hollered at her. She glanced down. Her belly seemed bigger than it had been before, but it had to be her imagination. Of course that's all it was.

10.

"Well, it's time. Cattle gotta go to market. We'll be leaving in a few days." Jarvis sat heavily in his chair. "Woman, this looks like a fine meal."

Mathilde stared into the distance.

"Woman, I told you this looks like a fine meal."

"I'm happy for you."

"What in the world is that supposed to mean?"

"You taught me to shoot, and this entire time, you still haven't looked at me. You haven't seen my face. And we sleep together, but we've never *slept* together. You say you were around a lot of ladies when you were younger. Could have fooled me! Something's wrong here, Jarvis. And the hands aren't much better!"

"What's wrong with the hands?" His voice had a little heat to it.

"Nothing wrong. They just... I don't know. They're ignoring their wives, it sounds like. And there's something wrong with the girls, too."

"Oh?"

She chewed her lip. How was all this coming out now? "They're all putting on weight."

"Eating proper will do that to a woman."

She looked down at herself. Her breasts were practically falling out of her dress, she'd grown so much. "Not like this, Jarvis. Something's wrong."

He raised an eyebrow toward the distant wall. "So what do you want? Want me to throw the dishes off the table, tear your dress off, and have my way with you? Treat you like a belonging, like I should do whatever I want to you? Treat you like I treat the animals?"

Now heat reached her cheeks. "At least you treat the animals out there like you care for them!"

He blinked, glanced past her, and then back to the far wall. "Maybe I've done you wrong, woman. I'll send you back east if you want, after I get back from the trail. Won't be gone but a month or two."

"I don't want to go back east!" She pounded the table and stood. "I want to be your wife! That's what I signed up for!"

Jarvis's chair scraped against the floor. He stood. "Woman, that's enough of that. I signed that contract, too. I'm the one who wanted you out here. I'm sorry I'm not enough of a man for you. If you want, I can give you to one of the hands. I'm sure they'd breed you silly if you wanted. I figured you for someone better than that. I wanted someone to keep me company. You've done that appreciably. You've learned how to handle a shotgun. But if you want someone to just take you out and breed you, look you in the eyes and call you by name like I call the cattle, well, you need another man."

His footsteps echoed as he left the dining room and made his way up the stairs.

Mathilde squeezed her eyes shut. Her shoulders shook.

This was supposed to be a new life. A good one. And Jarvis was good. He wasn't taking anything from her. Why was she so upset?

Why wouldn't he look at her?

His footsteps echoed down the upstairs hallway. He'd walked past their bedroom. A key slid into a lock. A door opened.

Something moved in his office.

Mathilde frowned. He was in his office? He never went in there. At least, she'd never noticed him go in there before. Maybe he had some sort of paperwork to do before hitting the trail. That would make sense.

And then his gruff voice murmured. She couldn't make out the words, but he was definitely talking to someone.

The door shut. The lock clicked. Jarvis made his way to their bedroom.

And Mathilde stood at the dining room table, alone.

11.

Two days later, Jarvis gathered the hands at dawn. They set out on their horses as the sun stretched their shadows long. Mathilde waved, along with the rest of the girls. Tears streaked Carrie's face.

Mathilde couldn't help but notice they didn't take all the cattle with them, though. The one Jarvis had paid attention to still stood in the yard, watching the men ride off. All the cattle were watching, actually. She narrowed her eyes. That was the one that Carrie's husband paid the most attention to. And wasn't that the one Annie had pointed out?

They'd left behind their favorite cows. Well, that made some sense, at least. If they cared for those cows so much, they wouldn't want to take them to the slaughterhouse.

But what made these cattle so important?

She waddled over to Jarvis's cow. She'd been feeling so bloated. The dresses hardly seemed to fit at all anymore. She patted the cow's back. It turned to look at her. Its eyes were still so, so sad.

"Well," she breathed, "It's just us ladies now."

As the sun rose higher, she fed the chickens and took their eggs. As she hefted the basket into the kitchen, something shifted in the house. The walls creaked constantly, it seemed.

A chair rubbed against the floor.

Mathilde frowned. "Hello?"

No answer.

She set the basket on the counter and moved into the dining room. No one here. She hadn't heard any of the doors bang. The girls didn't come up into the house. They stayed out by their husbands. No one else was supposed to be here.

It must have been her imagination. Of course it was.

A chair rubbed against the floor again. No, maybe it was something else. It wasn't in the dining room, that was for sure. It sounded like it was coming from upstairs. She made her way to the stairs and gazed up toward the bedroom. "Hello?"

Something moved up there.

Probably just a squirrel, right? Some other critter? That's why Jarvis had taught her how to use the shotgun. But it wouldn't be anything big. Couldn't be. Not up there. Just something that got in through the attic. All she had to do was walk up the steps, and whatever it was would scurry away. No reason to get excited. Jarvis had just left an hour ago. She shouldn't be nervous already!

Outside, all the cattle mooed. It was a lonesome, haunting sound. It sounded close, too, not just out in the yard. It sounded like it came from upstairs. Just a trick of the house, of course. It couldn't be anything else.

She forced herself to chuckle and trot up the steps. Whatever the critter was, it shouldn't be in the house. Ignore the cattle. They were just odd, that was all. She threw open the doors to the bedroom. Nothing scurried away. She didn't hear the tiny tapping of claws. Whatever it was, it wasn't in here.

She stepped back out and headed toward the hallway.

And then she froze. Something moved in the office.

"Hello?" she called.

A voice came from beyond the locked door. It sounded muffled, but not as if something was covering someone's mouth. More like the person's lips weren't working quite right. A little like they might be drunk, but still not quite right. "Please let me out." It sounded like a woman, but a woman with a deep voice. "Please let me out. I just want to go home."

"Who are you?" Mathilde gasped.

The woman on the other side of the door sobbed.

"Just wait. I don't know who you are, but you won't stay in there." She hurried to the staircase.

She froze at the top. She frowned. What was going on? Her legs locked up, like she'd forgotten how to walk down the stairs.

This was no time to be silly. Whatever was happening, whoever that girl was, it must be why Jarvis didn't want her going into that room. Mathilde had a feeling that everything that was wrong at the ranch, she'd figure it out if she could talk to that woman. Maybe Jarvis wasn't nearly as honorable as he tried to make out.

With a grunt, she forced herself to walk down the stairs. All she had to do was get into the room. And maybe Carrie would be able to get her in.

12.

Mathilde crossed the yard. All the cows watched her as she passed. She made it to the house Carrie stayed in and banged on the door. As she did, she noticed her knuckles were sore. "Carrie?" she called. "I need some help getting into a room in the house. Can you help?"

Inside, someone sobbed.

"Carrie?"

The crying continued.

She pushed the door open and snuck inside. It smelled like liquor and sweaty clothes. It was just one room, with a bed pushed up in the corner. Dusty sunbeams lit the room in a kind of twilight. Someone large sat on the bed. Their legs didn't look quite right, and their body was thicker than most people's she'd ever seen. The figure stared at its hands in its lap.

"Where's Carrie?"

The figure looked up at Mathilde. "Something's wrong with my hands." Her voice was thick, but it was definitely Carrie.

Mathilde stepped deeper into the house. The figure raised her head. Even her face seemed thick. Her nose widened in a strange way. And her eyes—

What was wrong with her eyes?

"I can't bend my fingers no more, Mathilde. I can't bend them. And my dresses. What's wrong with me?"

And her dress was wrong. It was like her breasts had descended. They seemed to be closer to her stomach now. The fabric strained to hold her flesh. She extended her hands. "Look at my fingers, Mathilde."

She did. She gasped. The fingers were hard and almost shiny in the dim light. They were black.

The same black as Mathilde's fingernails.

She stepped back from her friend.

Carrie's wide mouth frowned. "What's wrong with your face?"

"My face?" She raised a hand to her cheek.

"You got hair all over it."

She felt soft bristles all over her cheek. Her hand shook. She glanced around for a mirror but didn't spot one in the little room. She noticed the back of her hand, though. Tiny white hair sprouted across the back of it. Not just her nails, but her fingertips were black now, too.

"Carrie. We're leaving. The men left some horses. We're riding away. Get the other women."

"I ain't seen them. They're all staying in their houses."

"Get them. I'm going back into the house. There's someone in there. Someone trapped. I'm getting them out, and then we're leaving. To hell with whatever contracts we signed." The door banged as she rushed out.

The cows watched as she passed through the yard.

13.

Mathilde raced up the steps and flew to the office door. She tried the knob. Yep. Still locked.

"Is it you again?" the voice called out from inside.

"Yeah. Trying to figure out how to get you out." She gazed around at the door. She'd never been handy with tools, but there should be some way to get in there, right? "Who are you?"

"Maria. I'm Jarvis's wife."

The words slapped Mathilde. She took a step back from the door, her hands shaking. She had to find her breath again. "Who?"

"Maria. He brought me out here when he started the ranch. Years ago, I think. It's so hard to tell. But something went wrong. I don't know. My dresses got tight. And my fingers stopped working." She sobbed. "He stopped wanting to be with me. Said I looked like an animal."

"What happened to you?"

"Is it happening to you, too? Your voice sounds different. Like mine did."

Mathilde shook her head. No. No, it was not happening to her. She wouldn't let it, whatever it was. Whatever Jarvis was doing. His first wife? He never said anything about another woman. Was that why he wouldn't sleep with her? He just brought her out so that this thing would happen again?

All the cows in the yard mooed.

"Do you hear them?" Maria asked. "All the other girls."

"The other girls?" Her voice shook.

"Yeah. Out in the yard. He lets them out."

The other girls. The cows. The ones that Jarvis treated so well. The ones that the hands cared about.

"It's happening to you, too, isn't it?" Maria asked.

She glanced down at her body. Everything was shifting. She tripped over her own feet.

"Go. Just run. It's too late for me. It's already happened. Maybe you can save yourself. Go!"

Mathilde shook her head. No. She wasn't going to abandon this woman. The first woman Jarvis tricked. No. There was some way through this door. She ran against it. She pounded on it. There had to be some way.

Of course there was. The shotgun.

She rushed to the bedroom. It sat by her side of the bed,

propped up against the dresser. She plucked it up.

It clattered to the ground.

Her fingers. They weren't moving anymore. They were hard, so hard. Her elbows, too. They weren't bending the way they were supposed to. Her skin felt *wrong*. And hair. Hair all over. Patches of white and brown hair all over her arms.

She snatched the shotgun, balancing it in her arms. One shot, the door would fly open. Then they'd get the hell out. "Get away from the door! I'm getting you out of there!" Her voice. It was so deep.

Her fingers still wouldn't bend. She concentrated. Just one shot. That's all it would take.

Mathilde fell over. She pushed herself up, but her hips weren't working. She couldn't stand up.

Didn't matter right now. She slotted a thickening finger through the trigger. She pulled. The door flew open.

Inside stood a cow in the tatters of a woman's dress.

14.

Jarvis and the hands rode back to the house. The boys hollered for their wives. They had gotten money and bought all sorts of new things for the women. Dresses, mirrors, all the sorts of things they thought the women might like.

Jarvis didn't celebrate, though. He frowned as he gazed at the yard. More cows grazed there than when they'd left.

He dismounted and climbed the stairs into the house. He heard sounds upstairs in the office. He frowned as he came into sight of the broken door. Two cows looked up at him.

"Oh, Mathilde. I'd hoped we'd have more time together. Everyone ends up like Maria, though." He shook his head. "Guess I'll have to find another wife."

UNTIL DEATH

1.

The explosion knocked Sheriff Carter off his feet. His shoulder impacted the dusty road. He rolled, pulled his pistol from its holster, and pointed it at the sky as he rocked into a crouch, ready to fire at whoever needed to be shot today.

The front of Danzig's was fire and splinters. It smelled like burning kerosene and flesh. The heat was probably blistering his face already.

No time to shoot anyone right now. He had to get anyone in there out before the flames got worse. He holstered the pistol and sprinted for the store. The heat grew more intense as he got closer. He raised his arm to shield his face. Bart and Hilda were probably still in there. Any customers?

He glanced back. The townsfolk were starting to assemble. Bucket brigade would be starting up in just a minute. Probably too late for Danzig's, but hopefully they'd be able to protect the rest of the town from the flames. Wet the neighboring buildings down. Not his problem right now, though. He took one last breath and rushed through what remained of the front door.

Flames everywhere. Smoke stung his eyes. His lungs seemed to be on fire. So, so hot. So hard to breathe.

He pushed through to the counter. One of them was probably back there. He passed shelves filled with flour, sugar, all the normal things. And all the other stuff that Bart always brought to town. The weird stuff. He ignored it all.

There. The counter. He ran around it. Bart lay on the ground.

Half his face was bloody. Carter crouched over the general store owner. "Bart!" he screamed, trying to be louder than the fire and mostly failing.

"They stole it," the old man muttered. Chunks of his trimmed white beard dripped red. His eyes were glazed, but open. And if he was talking, obviously he wasn't dead yet. Probably.

Carter grabbed Bart's arm and pulled him up. The man collapsed, his legs boneless. "Not good enough," the sheriff muttered and wrapped the man's arm around his shoulder. "We gotta get you outta here so I can come back for your girl."

"I ain't got no girl," the store owner muttered. "They stole it."

"They took your girl?" He puffed, trying to get enough air into his lungs. There wasn't enough air in here. Bart's daughter was plenty pretty. 'Course a man would steal her.

A chunk of flaming ceiling fell in front of them. Carter kicked it out of the way and took another few steps. Bart's feet dragged across the floor.

"No. They took her skull."

He blinked. He took another few steps. They weren't going to make it out of here before he had burns all over his body, were they?

To hell with that. He'd lived in this town most of his life. He'd "won" the job of sheriff just a few months back. He wasn't going to let some fire kill him. Not today.

Another few steps as he tottered under the load. Bart remained limp. The door wasn't that far away. He couldn't fill his lungs, though. There wasn't enough air in here. Just smoke and death. Carter shook his head and immediately regretted it. The floor seemed to lurch under him. His sleeves burned his arms.

More steps. Not many at all. He could do this. He could get Bart out. He wasn't going to let the old man die.

Finally, they pushed through into the open air. He stumbled down the few steps from the patio to the street. He collapsed onto his knees. Bart fell like a sack of nails to the ground. Carter sucked in clean air.

He breathed in water. He spluttered and blinked.

"Sorry, Sheriff. Looked like you needed it."

He peered up at Doc Jasper. He held a dripping bucket. "Saw you coming. Figured you'd need to cool off."

Carter nodded and stumbled to his feet. "Help Bart. He's not doing good."

"Neither are you."

"Don't matter. Hilda's still in there. I gotta go back in."

"You go in there, you ain't coming back out. That fire's too hot."

"Don't matter none. I ain't leaving that girl in there by herself." He sucked in clean air and, before he could think enough to regret it, ran back into the remains of the general store.

2.

Glass exploded somewhere to his right. Timbers creaked deeper in the store. The smoke hung thicker in the air. Carter pulled the handkerchief from his back pocket. It was soaked from Doc Jasper's splash of water. Good thing. He held it over his nose and tried to breathe clean air.

Bart's daughter was probably in the back. It's where she usually was if she wasn't behind the counter. That's great. He just had to get through the front.

He didn't let himself think. He ran around the counter and through the door to the back room.

All four walls were nothing but flames. At least one of the ceiling supports had given way. Bags of flour burned bright. Sugar bags flowed with scalding black caramel. More glass popped. Corn exploded.

And standing in the middle of the room, her fists clenched at her sides, stood Hilda Danzig, Bart's daughter. She was maybe sixteen with long dark hair and a thin figure. Right now, she spat at the walls.

Great. The fire must have turned her around or something. He'd heard of such things. The smoke got in your head, and you couldn't find the way out of the house you'd always lived in. Carter snatched her elbow.

She spun and slapped him across the jaw. He landed on the floor. The girl had more spice in her than he would have expected. That was probably good for her. She needed it for as many boys came sniffing around her. Carter wasn't interested in someone so young, though.

He struggled to get to his knees. "Hilda!" he yelled.

She shook her head, eyes focusing on him. "Sheriff!" she screamed. "You need to get out of here!"

"You're a genius!" He grabbed her elbow again and pulled. At least he didn't need to carry her out.

"Go! I need to get something!" She moved toward a wall of fire.

"No! You're coming with me!"

She screamed some more things. She yanked against him.

They didn't have time for this. He swept an arm behind her legs and lifted her. She kicked. She spat. It was like trying to carry a wildcat, claws and all. At least she was lighter than Bart.

Carter spun to get out of the back room, but he lost sight of the door. It had to be this direction, though. Where else would it be? He pushed forward and nearly ran into a wall. Where was the door?

Oh. Great. Now he was the one turned around. Of course he was.

The ceiling creaked. The entire building was going to come down any moment, right on top of them. That would be great. Sheriff Carter, dead at thirty-seven. He survived all the creepy stuff of the town but couldn't handle rescuing a little girl. Fantastic. It's how he'd always dreamed he'd die.

Hilda kept fighting.

"Girl, calm down! I'm trying to get you to safety!" He paced along the wall. That should lead to a door eventually, right? The back room couldn't be that big.

Hilda didn't calm down. How was it women folk never listened when he told them to calm down? And how big was it back here? It felt like he'd been walking far enough to get to his office from Danzig's. He staggered.

"Put me down!" the girl shrieked.

"Fine!" He put her on her feet.

She snagged his hand. "Come on!" She pushed deeper into the smoke.

And then they stepped out of the general store and onto the main street of town, as if they hadn't been in any danger at all. Looking at her, she didn't look like she'd been in any trouble. Her hair didn't even look mussed.

Well, that was fine. He'd rescued her, right?

Doc Jasper splashed him with another bucket of water.

3.

It hurt to sit.

Sheriff Carter tried ignoring the pain. He had things to do. Didn't matter how much of him was burned. He had to investigate, and that probably meant he'd uncover more weirdness. It'd be so much better if it was just bandits. Bullets he could deal with. Weird stuff? Not so much.

Doc Jasper crossed his arms. "You're supposed to be lying down."

"Yep."

"You got as many burns as Bart does. He's still lying down."

"Yep."

"You're twice as stubborn as I am."

"Yep." Carter arched his back to stretch and immediately regretted it. "Don't tell me, Doc. I know. If I was lying down, I'd be getting better so much faster."

The huge man shrugged. "You want to get an infection, well, I guess Clive can take care of you after that. I'm sure he can dress you up nice after you die. Parson can bury you then."

Carter ignored the comments. "Bart ready for some questions?"

"Sure. It won't hurt him none. Not so sure he'll be able to answer, though, with how much laudanum I gave him. Might take him so long to recover you might as well go lay down." Jasper leaned forward onto Carter's desk. "And wouldn't that be a shame."

"Someone blew up Danzig's. I need to find them."

"Bart's always bringing in creepy stuff. He probably got some bomb and it finally exploded."

"But I won't know that until he wakes up."

"You could always talk to Hilda."

"How's she doing?"

"Not a single burn. She didn't even smell like smoke. She's lucky to be alive, all things concerned."

Carter nodded. "Fine." He shifted in his chair and winced.

"You wouldn't mind bringing her here, would you?"

Jasper snorted and left the office.

It had only been a few hours, but they'd been able to keep the blaze from spreading. The town splashed the surrounding buildings with enough water that nothing else burned down. Just their general store. That was fine. Bart made enough he should be able to rebuild. The town needed that place, or one like it.

Hilda stormed into the office not too long after Doc Jasper headed out. "You wanted to see me?" She crossed her arms and tapped her toe. The scar under her left eye blazed, just like it always did when she was emotional. Kevin Vintner tried courting her last spring, and she looked just like that. Kevin never came around town any more after whatever she said to him; he stayed out at Jarvis's ranch.

"Yeah. Have a seat, darling." Carter gestured to a chair on the other side of his desk.

"I'm not your darling." Her voice was like ice, but she sat.

"You ain't much of anyone's darling except Bart's." He tried shrugging, but his skin was too stiff. He sighed instead. "Your dad should be fine, though, from what Doc Jasper was saying."

She continued watching him.

"So your store blew up. Any idea why?"

"Two people came in. They knew what they were looking for. Gaagii's Skull. I brought it here because it was the only place they wouldn't be able to find it."

Carter blinked. Weird stuff. Yep. Always the weird stuff. "A skull?"

"Doesn't matter except we need it back. You'll get it for me, right, Sheriff Carter?" Her voice lightened. Something in her shifted. She didn't look like some kid now. She looked closer to his age, more filled out in the right places.

Carter frowned and leaned away from her. His back grazed the chair and screamed out in pain. He grimaced. "I'll do what I can to make it right," he gritted out. "A skull, though?"

"Just a skull. Looks like any human's skull. You wouldn't be able to tell it apart from any other. It's... important, though." Something in her clothing shifted. He could see down the front of her dress far more than was appropriate.

He cleared his throat and looked away. "What can you tell me about the two people who took it?"

"They knew exactly what they were looking for. Didn't demand cash or any supplies. Just the skull. It was a man and a woman. He was huge and carried a lot of equipment. She was smaller, but obviously the brains between the two of them."

Carter swore. That sounded like Vera and Volcano. They were wanted all over the state. He'd wanted bandits. Now he had them, and the weird shit, too.

4.

Early the next morning Carter rode out of town on Jacob's back. By the time he'd finished talking to Greta, it was late enough he knew he'd have to wait. Sleep didn't come easily with the burns, but at least he rested some. Now, with the sun breaking the horizon behind him, he rode west. His shadow stretched on the flat sands.

They weren't even trying to hide where they'd gone. Hoofprints had thrown up the dirt as they'd scrambled away.

Just him against two of them. Maybe he should have deputized someone and brought them along, but he hated doing that ever since Vince had been shot up a couple months back. Better that he just took care of himself and didn't have to worry about anyone else. He'd think of something. He always did.

He rode due west until the sun burned red on the distant horizon. By then he'd come to the hills. He lit a fire and camped overnight. His back kept him from sleeping well.

At dawn he set out through the hills. At first, they rose in gentle swells, and then stones broke through the dirt. Soon enough he'd be entering the mountains.

And still the trail was fairly easy to follow. He had no doubt they'd come this way. Cigarette butts littered the ground. Plenty of disturbed dirt. And no one came out this way. The ranchers stayed away from the hills. No natives lived anywhere near Scar Ridge. No, he was definitely still following the bandits.

Jacob had sure feet even through the wilderness. Carter appreciated that in a horse.

Today was hotter. Sweat dripped down his face. His back

burned. He wished that it was something that had just exploded. If it hadn't been bandits, he could be back home resting. Well, that's why he got paid. Had to hunt down vermin like this.

At sunset he spotted a flickering fire in the shadow of the mountains. He rode toward it. As he drew closer, he spotted a large man tending the flames. A shorter woman leaned against her pack, her arms behind her head. A lazy smile played across her face. As he rode up, she stood and touched a finger to her hat. "Hey. Little late to be riding by yourself through the wilds."

He nodded. "It is at that."

"Come join us by the fire." She gestured. "Name's Vera. That there's my partner, Volcano."

The man continued tending the flames. He grunted.

He nodded back. "Carter. I'm the sheriff of Scar Ridge. Looking for some folk that caused a mess in town two days back."

"Sounds like a brave thing to do on your lonesome." She put her hands on her hips, close enough to the pistols holstered there. "Either that or a foolish thing."

"I've been accused of one more than the other." They could take him easily. Might as well take advantage of the offered hospitality. He dismounted with a groan. "But it'd be good to sit by the fire with you." He made sure to keep his hands away from his guns.

"We've got some tinned beans warming up," Vera said. "Take care of your horse and join us."

He did just that, making sure Jacob had plenty of space to get whatever greenery he could find. Carter grabbed out a tin plate and a fork from his pack and approached the fire. Volcano raised an eyebrow and a steaming can from where it'd been heating up among the coals. The sheriff proffered his plate, and soon he had beans to devour.

He plunked himself down on the ground. "You two blew up a fine general store."

The huge man rumbled a deep laugh.

Vera shrugged. "My partner can be a little eager with the fireworks."

He shoveled some food into his gob. "You've got some skull?"

"Yep. That was the job. Find the skull, bring it out of Scar Ridge. Anyone die back there? We only kill people we're hired to kill."

"That remains to be seen." Carter kept his voice even. Sure, Hilda was fine, but Bart could still get a nasty infection from the burns. So could he, but he ignored that part of it. "It would be a shame if I had to hunt you down for manslaughter."

"Maybe I should tell you we've been hired to kill anyone who gets in our way." Vera ate some of her own beans. "We'd hate to shoot you, Sheriff. You're not part of the job."

He sighed. "I'd hate to be shot, especially by someone who's feeding me."

"You bring any whiskey with you?"

He groaned as he stood and moved to his pack, retrieving a flask. He took a pull and passed it to Vera. She took her own pull and handed it to Volcano, who drank deeply and didn't pass it on.

Carter pressed his lips together. "Got that flask from my brother."

Volcano raised an eyebrow, took another deep pull, and tossed it to him empty.

"I'm not fond of weirdness. Don't want much to do with a skull. But you did steal it from someone in my town. And blew up a building." He pocketed the flask.

Vera shrugged. "And you want justice done, I'm sure."

"I am rather fond of justice."

She chuckled. "You ain't gonna find it here, Sheriff. If you reach for your guns, you'll be dead before you draw."

"And it ain't exactly polite to shoot someone who fed you." He nodded to his plate of beans. "Mind if I tag along with you to whoever hired you? Maybe I can talk some sense into them."

Vera and Volcano glanced at each other. The huge man shrugged. Vera sighed. "As long as we get paid, that's all we care about. Come on with, Sheriff. We won't shoot you in the back as long as you don't shoot us."

5.

Carter woke up alive. He appreciated that. The two bandits could have easily killed him in the night, but they chose not to. He climbed out of his bed roll and packed up.

Volcano stretched and lumbered off to relieve himself. Vera packed up their end of the camp. Soon enough the three of them rode toward the top of the ridge.

"Where you meeting up with the party that hired you?" Carter asked.

Vera nodded toward the rise. "Just outside Scar Ridge territory."

"Didn't want to come over here?"

She shrugged. "They said they didn't know where the town was. Just said the skull had been taken to Danzig's. It was hard enough finding our own way there."

The sheriff frowned. "They couldn't find the town?" He turned in the saddle. "It's just back there." Memories of a town that had vanished flickered through his mind.

"I know. But you can't always find it from outside." She shook her head. "You got a weird place back there, Sheriff."

"I know. Trust me, I know."

A few hours later the horses crossed over the top of the ridge and began descending through the rocky space. They moved through a stony ravine.

Carter glanced around. "I didn't realize there were mines along here." He eyed some of the dark openings that popped up occasionally in the cliffsides.

"They ain't been used in years. No one ever found anything worthwhile."

"Why bother digging then?"

"Why'd someone build a town in the middle of nowhere?" Vera chuckled. "You ain't got nothing there. No rail line. No mines. Some ranches, sure, but nothing worth building a town around. Sometimes people just don't make sense, Sheriff."

"There you and I have to agree." He sighed. It was shaping up to be a hot one again. "How'd you two end up together?"

"Volcano whispered some poetry in my ear."

The man rumbled a laugh.

A gunshot echoed. Splinters of rock flew up beside Carter. He dove off his horse and scrambled to a boulder for cover.

Vera raised a hand. "Got your skull!" she shouted.

Gunshots answered her. She launched herself from her saddle and took cover next to Carter. Volcano joined them a heartbeat later. Each of them held their pistols.

"Friends of yours?" Carter asked.

"Only people who knew we'd be here were the ones who hired us." She narrowed her eyes. "I don't much appreciate people shooting at me when they should be paying me."

"Who hired you?" He gritted his teeth. He really didn't want to have to make a stand with these two.

"Indians. They wanted the skull back."

"Back?"

"I didn't ask." She glanced up over the boulder and ducked when more gunshots rang out. "I'll cover you two. Try to get up on top of the ravine. You'll be able to shoot down at them then."

Volcano grunted agreement.

"Yeah sure. I didn't want to live until the end of today," Carter muttered.

Vera grabbed the back of Volcano's neck and brought his lips to hers. They parted, stared into each other's eyes, and shouted, "Till death!"

"Yeah. Sure." Carter glanced up at the ravine walls. "That way?"

Vera shot over the boulder, and Volcano and Carter charged up the ravine wall.

6.

Carter flattened himself as more shots rang out. Rocks splintered around him. "I thought she was supposed to be covering us!"

Volcano chuckled and slapped him on the back.

Carter bit back a cry of pain. Stupid burns. He didn't have time to hurt. Not if he was going to avoid getting shot, which would be his preference. He pushed through the pain and kept scrambling up the slope, doing his best to dodge behind the various stony outcroppings.

He really wanted to shoot back. They better not hit Jacob. That was a good horse. It looked like all three horses were well-trained animals, though. They milled around but didn't panic. None of them had been hit, either. The natives out there must be wanting them for themselves, then. Well, at least for now, that was good for the horses.

He threw himself behind another boulder. More bullets splintered the rock. He gasped for breath. How much longer until the top of the slope?

Way too far. That's how long. Of course it was.

He raised his head to peak over the edge of the stone and ducked as quickly as he could. He still couldn't spot whoever was shooting at them. Maybe it was natives, but they never bothered anyone in Scar Ridge. Why bother someone here right at the border of their territory? It didn't make any sense.

He gasped for breath and just kept reminding himself at least this wasn't anything weird. Just bullets. Bullets he could handle, as long as they weren't going through his skin. Just people over there. It wasn't someone out to eat his bones or collect his eyes or anything else that happened back in town. Just people trying to kill him in the old-fashioned way.

Still meant he could die, of course, and that really wasn't his preference.

He shook himself and pushed up the ravine wall again. Another boulder. Another. He dodged. He took cover. Nothing hit him, though he swore he felt the wind of passing bullets. Sweat stung his eyes. Stone dug into his fingers, leaving bloody cuts.

There. Finally. He hauled himself up a stone shelf, yanking his legs after him and rolling out of sight. He'd made it to the top of the ridge. No one could fire down at him here. He panted for a moment before climbing into a crouch. He scanned the area.

Volcano crept along the top of the ravine, his eyes locked somewhere ahead and a little down. Carter followed his gaze. A group of five natives crouched behind a line of stone, firing at Vera. Two sighted down rifles, waiting for her to appear. A few pointed up at the top of the ravine. One fired a pistol. Carter threw himself to the ground. The bullet went wide.

The huge man glanced back at the sheriff. He offered a mad grin and swung something off his back.

Carter gasped. A portable mortar? Volcano set it on the ground and tinkered with it, looking down at the natives. His tongue stuck out the corner of his mouth.

There was no way the natives would be able to survive that. Carter'd seen what a mortar could do to a human body. Sure, they started this. They'd fired on the people they'd hired to get the skull. But to fire a mortar? "Just scare them off, right?" His voice felt scratchy.

"They hired us. Want to kill us now?" Volcano answered.

"You talk?" Carter didn't know how to react.

"This'll mess them up." He wiped sweat from his forehead.

"Look, just scare them off, all right? No reason to kill them all."

"I do that, they shoot us all. We're dead." He reached for the mortar to drop into the metal pipe.

Carter threw the first punch. Probably should have drawn his pistol instead. One on one, he could take down just about anyone. Vera wasn't here to back her partner up. He wasn't thinking about that right then, though. There was a reason he was sheriff and not in charge of the bank. Honestly, he probably shouldn't be the sheriff at all.

His fist connected with Volcano's jaw. He didn't even flinch. Carter dodged the uppercut and went for his gut. Volcano lashed out, taking the sheriff in his side. The breath whooshed out of him. He ducked under the huge man's swipe but couldn't avoid the punch that took him in the jaw. He landed on the ridge hard.

Volcano grunted and turned back to the mortar and lit it. Carter kicked out, knocking one of the legs out right as a sparking fire burst from the metal pipe. It arced through the sky and landed next to the natives.

The blast rocked the hills. Pebbles skittered down the side of the ravine. Men shouted in surprise and anger. Carter rolled over to peer down. Four men fled. One remained behind, holding a hand to his bloody face.

7.

Stones scattered around Carter as he skidded down the ravine's wall. Volcano shouted after him, but he paid no attention. Vera watched his descent, her hands on her hips. The sheriff rushed to the native's side.

The mortar had banged him up badly. His entire side was bloody. He heaved for breath. "Where'd you come from?" he spoke in carefully enunciated English. "We watched. The hunters disappeared when we hired them. They came back from nowhere."

Carter pressed his lips together. No amount of bandaging was going to help this man. He was going to be dead soon.

"The skull?"

"You just tried killing the people you hired to get it."

"The girl. With the scar under her left eye. She stole it when my grandfather was young. We finally heard it had found its way to your town." He gasped for breath. "It's evil. Taints whoever's near it. We have to destroy it. You were carrying it. You're tainted. You must die."

Stones scattered nearby. Volcano slid to a stop and ambled over to them. He grunted, glaring down at the native.

The wounded man's eyes widened. "The skull!" he shouted.

Before Carter realized what was happening, Volcano lifted his foot and smashed it down on the native's face. Bones crunched. He kicked again. A third time. Gore splattered. The huge man bellowed a hearty laugh.

The sheriff shook himself. He stood and drew his pistol.

Volcano grinned and turned on Carter.

"Back down!" Vera's command echoed off the stony walls. Both men froze. They faced each other, but their eyes darted to her. Her pistol was aimed right at Volcano. "You didn't have to do that." Her voice came so soft now, so remorseful. "Vol, honey, what'd you do that for?"

His throaty chuckle answered her. Flies buzzed around the blood on his boot. He turned his shoulders to face her and trodded toward his woman, hands out as if to take her by the shoulders. Something in his gaze threatened violence.

"Back off." Carter found his voice, his own pistol aimed squarely at the huge man. "You stay away from her."

"Don't you threaten my man." Now Vera's Colt turned on the lawman. "We can take care of ourselves."

Great. Two against one, maybe? All he wanted was to return the skull to town. To hell with these two. Keep the gun aimed at Volcano, or turn it on her? He took a deep breath and lifted his barrel to point at the sky. "No threats here."

A growl started deep in Volcano's throat.

"He's got the skull?" Carter nodded toward him. "The native he killed said the skull corrupted people. That's why they were shooting at us." More weirdness. He hated it, but he'd learned to trust it, too. Or at least, not second-guess people who seemed to know what they were talking about. "They thought we were corrupted."

Volcano lunged at him. He threw himself backwards, his gun pointing toward the huge man. He fired once, twice. Landed on his back. Pain shot through his skin and muscles from the burns. He cried out. The huge man landed on top of him. Blood poured down his left arm, but he didn't even seem to notice. His hands gripped either side of Carter's face and squeezed. Pressure built around his skull. He slammed the grip of his pistol against Volcano's temple. The man didn't move. He slammed again.

The pressure released. The weight vanished. Volcano rolled to the side. Vera screamed at him, but Carter wasn't paying much attention. He couldn't hear over the sound of the blood in his ears. He coughed and rolled off his back. He might not be able to stand. So, so much pain.

The woman kicked her man in the ribs, shouting something indecipherable. Carter blinked his vision clear and peered over at them. Volcano laughed as she beat him.

Flies buzzed everywhere. Where'd they come from? He glanced over at the dead native. His crushed face was already alive with maggots. Carter gagged. A fly landed on him. He waved it away. Another two, three came his way.

And then he noticed the blood that dripped down Volcano's arm. It, too, moved with the wriggling motion of maggots.

He vomited. He couldn't keep anything inside of him. Once he'd emptied three lawmen's worth of stomachs, he lurched to his feet and trained his gun on the huge man. "Vera, back off." His voice sounded rough in his ears.

"You stay out of this!"

"Something's wrong here. Weird. Look at him. He ain't the man I rode with earlier today."

She turned on him. The second she did, Volcano reached out and yanked on her ankle. She fell to the ground. He raised a fist high in the air to pound her.

Carter fired. He knew his pistol. Even beat up and weak as he was, he knew where that bullet went. Volcano didn't even flinch, though. His fist rocketed like a mortar into Vera's face. She cried out in pain. Then she gurgled.

What was it going to take to put this man down?

Where was the skull? If that was the problem, all he had to do was destroy the skull, right? That's how weird things were supposed to work. Should be easy. Was it in his pack? He'd worn that thing constantly. It's where the mortar had come from. It was still slung on his back.

Carter tackled the huge man. He didn't shift under the weight. That was fine. Carter wasn't trying to take him down, really. He snatched at the pack.

Volcano spun then. At least he wasn't beating Vera anymore. A fist like a blacksmith's hammer collided with Carter's ribs. His vision went dark for a second. Still, he clung to the pack. If he could get the skull out, if that's what was causing all this, maybe he could get Volcano back to his usual bandit self, not this monster.

And that's when the natives started shooting again.

8.

All three of them flung themselves against the ravine's wall. Bullets flew thicker than before. Carter pressed himself against the stone and gasped for breath, holding back the pain that rolled through his body. Volcano dripped blood next to him. Vera glared at her partner. "What did you think you were doing?" she hissed.

He growled in answer.

"Don't do that to me! We're partners! Until death!"

His hands curled into meaty, bloody fists. Flies buzzed around them. Maggots wormed through his beard.

Carter flinched. That bullet was closer than he'd prefer. "We can't stay here."

"Mortar would've taken care of them," Volcano ground out.

"Yeah. Probably." He nodded to the other side of the ravine. "Take a look over there. A mine entrance. Plenty of cover. We'll be safe if we can make it."

"You're crazy, Sheriff," Vera breathed.

"Probably. Even crazy people like staying alive, though." He raised his head to try to spot where the natives were shooting from. "I'm going to start firing. Hopefully that'll give us enough cover to get to the mine."

"We'll be with you," Vera said.

"I'd appreciate you waiting to kill me until they're done shooting." He took a deep breath. His burns screamed at him. His gut protested where Volcano struck him. Wasn't time for any of that, though. "Let's do this." He fired from where he sheltered once, twice, then stepped out and fired again toward where he thought the natives might be.

Vera stepped out behind him and fired past him. Volcano followed suit. Bullets whistled past. Carter fired again and dashed toward the open mouth of the manmade cave. His back screamed at him. Hopefully it wasn't a bullet on top of everything else. He fired wildly twice more, emptying his pistol. He dove into the shadow.

Safe.

Not even half a breath later, Vera and Volcano made it to cover. They all gasped as the gunshots continued outside. They leaned against the timbers that held up the ceiling. Dust sprinkled down on them.

Carter emptied the cartridges from his pistol and reloaded as quickly as he could. His hands shook, but that didn't bother him much. He'd had to reload with shaking hands more than once before.

Vera looked over at her man. "You look like hell."

He grinned. Something wriggled between his teeth. A lot of somethings.

She reached in for an embrace. He wrapped his arms around her. Carter wrinkled his nose. She could see the blood, the maggots, right? How could she not?

A blade tore through fabric. A bag flew through the air at him and thunked on the ground not far away. "Get the skull, Sheriff!"

Volcano roared. He flung Vera aside. She landed against the wall with a terrible crunching sound. Volcano scurried toward Carter on all fours. Foam dribbled down his beard.

Carter snatched the bag and turned it upside down. The

contents of the bag spread across the ground. Cartridges. Mortars. Jerky.

A skull.

Just a human skull. Nothing fancy. It didn't have horns. No strange marks. Just a bleached white skull, as plain as any other dead man's.

All he had to do was break it, right? That's how weird stuff worked. He just had to shatter it, and whatever was happening to Volcano would stop. And then the natives would back off, because their skull couldn't corrupt anyone. Simple.

Except Volcano collided with the sheriff and pinned him to the wall. Maggots fell from his hair and slithered over Carter's face. He gagged. His back. His face. All of him burned in pain. He pushed back, but the mountain of a man was too, too strong. Blood all over. He tried to point his pistol, but Volcano was inside his reach. He couldn't get a good shot.

He could shoot the ceiling though. Might bury them all.

He didn't much look forward to dying, but it might be the only way to take out Volcano and the skull. He struggled to point the gun up.

Something crackled. Volcano spun. Carter collapsed against the wall, trying not to sob in the sudden relief.

Vera stood next to the skull, one foot pressing down on it. Cracks formed across the white surface.

Volcano flung himself at her, an inhuman howl shattering the air.

Vera pounded on the skull again. It shattered.

Volcano roared in triumph. He grabbed Vera by the neck and hoisted her above his head. He slavered, "That witch put protections on the skull. Trapped me there. But now you freed me, little worm. Little, tasty worm. Dirt and dust." He licked her cheek. Squirming maggots dropped from his mouth in clumps. "He's mine now."

Carter gasped for air. Well, he was dead anyway, wasn't he? No way he was getting out of this alive. At least he could take some weirdness with him.

He fired at the ceiling.

9.

Dust and dirt and stones and boulders and death. It all fell on them. The last thing Carter saw was a stone the size of a horse land on Volcano's head. The man collapsed under the onslaught. 'Course, so did Carter. The roar was louder than fifteen mortars. He couldn't breathe.

Yep. This was the end.

He didn't know how long it was. He didn't know how long it took. He didn't want to think about how torn his hands were or how he was still alive. Maybe God smiled on him finally. It was about time, for the amount of justice Carter dealt out and how much he had to deal with. But somehow, he crawled out of the collapsed mine.

No natives waited for him. They'd even left the horses. Good thing. He dragged himself toward Jacob. All he wanted to do was go home. To hell with recovering the skull for Hilda. The bandits were taken care of. That's all that mattered.

Stones shifted behind him.

He turned to gaze over his shoulder. A small woman fell out of the mine. She curled in on herself and retched.

Carter pushed himself to sit up. He waited for her to recover. He should probably take her back, lock her up. She did blow up Danzig's.

She leaned against the ravine wall. Finally, she shoved herself to her feet. She drew her pistol. "He was my man. You killed him."

"Maybe it slipped your mind." His voice was a lot weaker than he wanted it to be, but hell, he'd been through enough. "Your man was trying to kill you."

She aimed the pistol at him. "Until death."

"You gonna shoot a man that's sitting on the ground?"

"Get up." She motioned with the gun. "Get up, Sheriff. Let me kill you on your feet."

He sighed. "It's gotta be this way?"

Her expression didn't change.

"Well." He used a boulder to leverage himself up. His hand shook. He'd been banged up so much in the last few hours. Now, was he going to get shot for all his troubles? He looked over at her. "Just go, all right? You've suffered enough. I won't chase after you."

"Like hell. Draw."

The gunshot echoed off the ravine walls.

10.

He buried her. Least he could do after all that. He mounted Jacob and led the other two horses home. With the skull gone, hopefully now the town could rein in the weird.

NOT QUITE A DEER

1.

Three nights without water. Silent lightning forked across the distant sky, so far away no one could hear the rumbling. The humid heat of the day refused to let up, even an hour after sunset. The herd was restless, refusing to bed down for the evening. The beef lowed at the heavens, shifting on their hooves. Most of the hands were circling the herd, trying to keep them contained. It wouldn't take much for them to stampede.

Micah shoveled steaming beans into his trap. Ben had set up the campfire like normal, of course, and the hands were eating in shifts. It would probably be another sleepless night, but the *segundo* was sure they'd make Hope River tomorrow. Once the herd was watered, everything should be easier.

"They're real loud tonight," Micah said between bites.

Ben looked out toward the herd, sweat dripping down his face. "I haven't seen beefs this restless in a long time."

"Oh?" Micah kept shoveling. The faster he ate, the faster the next hand could eat. They tried to help each other out as much as they could, especially at times like this.

Ben shook his head. "Hope it doesn't come to that."

"The herd's stampeded before. We've always got them back under control in a few miles." Micah shrugged.

Ben sniffed. "Hope so, Micah. Hope so."

The herd screamed. Every single one called out to the sky, all at once. Micah leaped to his feet, plate in hand. He couldn't hear anything over the beefs.

Silence.

The fire crackled.

Micah couldn't move. He hadn't heard silence on the trail like this ever. It didn't happen. There was always some fool beef making a racket. There were all the bugs chattering in the weeds. Coyotes. Something.

No. Nothing.

Ben swore. "Micah, you stay here. You don't want to be riding out there."

"Like hell." He set down the plate and dashed for his night horse, still saddled from when he rode in fifteen minutes ago for his supper.

The steady chestnut shied from his hand.

"Come on, boy," he chided the horse.

It stepped back, its eyes white. It snorted.

Micah lunged to seize the reins in his calloused hand and swung himself into the saddle. "Come on!" And they were off into the night, toward the herd.

After just a minute, he met up with Freeman. "What's going on?" Micah asked.

Freeman shook his head. "No idea. They just up and stopped. Look at them! They're ready to run, all right."

Lightning lit the sky in a silent flash.

"I'll circle the other way. You keep them calm," Micah said.

Freeman spat. "Boy, I've been on more trails than you and your brothers combined! I know my business."

Micah rode away without another word. Sure, it was his first trail, but he was no fool. He knew how to calm a herd. He knew how to rein in a stampede, too, but he didn't want to have to. He should pass one of the other riders soon enough. There were fourteen of them, and they should all be circling the herd.

He squinted ahead, trying to spy the next rider. He should be out there, somewhere. It was almost like he could see the silence, it was so thick. He rolled his shoulders.

His first ride, but he'd be fine. Of course he would.

He'd be fine.

2.

Micah's horse's hooves thudded against dirt and grass. The beef, though. Not a single beef laid down. Not one. Even after three days without water, they should be tired enough that at least some would be tuckered out. They weren't moving, either. They weren't shifting from hoof to hoof. They weren't flicking their ears. They stood still.

Micah's breath came short and fast. Sure, it was his first trail, but his family always had a few head of cattle. He knew what was normal. He'd never experienced anything like it, and he'd never heard about anything like it in the yarns around the campfire. His heart thudded hard in his chest.

Movement.

There. On the hill facing the herd. Silent lightning lit up the prairie. A shadow of movement before darkness returned.

Micah's hand shot to his pistol. Anything could make the herd run when it was this tense.

The back of his throat itched. They'd had to cut back on their water, too. His canteen had a few swallows of water in it yet.

What was out there? Hard to tell in the darkness from this distance. Probably not a rustler; didn't look human. Didn't look big enough to be a buffalo either, thank God.

Another flash of light.

Just a deer.

Micah breathed a sigh. Some of the tension fled from his shoulders, but the itch in the back of his throat grew in intensity. His hand slipped away from his pistol. A deer. It would probably scamper off, silent and quick. Shouldn't bother the herd at all.

Shouldn't.

But something about the deer stuck in his head. The flash of light was so brief, outlining slender legs, body, antlerless head.

Another flash.

It had moved closer to the herd. The thing was fast. It stood still in the brief brightness, its head turned toward Micah.

Did it only have two legs?

No. Must have been a trick of the light.

Micah's hand wandered toward his pistol again. Tension returned to stretch across his shoulders.

His horse shied.

"No, we're circling the herd. Ain't no deer going to scare us," he said. He hoped he convinced the horse.

The chestnut hesitated, then obeyed.

Maybe one of the other boys would be circling his way soon. Should be, at least. If they were all moving, he should be meeting one of the others pretty quick, right?

Usually they sang to the herd to keep the beef calm. No one was singing tonight, he realized.

Where were the bugs? Why weren't the cattle moving at all?

Another flash.

The deer stood not thirty feet away.

Just a deer.

No. It wasn't quite a deer. It had too many joints. No, not enough. Something about its legs. How many legs did it have?

It stared into Micah.

Darkness.

The beef stampeded.

3.

The thunder of hooves swelled. The ground trembled. A bevy of pistol shots fired into the air—a signal from the other boys so everyone could tell what direction the herd was running.

The herd ran from the deer.

From the thing that was like a deer.

From the whatever-it-was that was staring straight at Micah. Even though the darkness had swallowed the thing up, Micah was sure it was still there.

His horse shook under him, and not from exhaustion. Or maybe that was just Micah shaking. Hard to tell.

The herd thundered away. The boys would be chasing them, trying to take the lead, to rope off the leaders and control the run.

Here was Micah, terrified of a deer. Just a deer. That's all it was. That's all it could be. He'd heard stories, of course. They all told their stories around the fire at night. It's what they did on the trail. He'd heard about the dead, the ghosts, the bloody tales. He'd heard about the not-quite-men who stole boys from the trail so their women mourned them. He knew about all that.

Ain't no one told him about a deer.

He should turn the horse. He should chase after the herd. Help keep it together. Get it back under control.

He should.

He couldn't move his arms. He couldn't kick his heels.

The humid air pressed in on him, squeezing his chest. His heart fought back. Breathing was getting hard. He coughed. Something scratched the back of his throat. Some of the beans must have lodged there.

Lightning lit the prairie with its cold and sudden light.

The deer.

The not-quite-a-deer.

It stood right in front of him.

His horse bucked. It kicked and screamed.

Micah fell out of his saddle. He snatched at the reins as he fell. They slipped from his fingers. His left foot tangled in a stirrup. Didn't matter. He was out of the saddle, and his horse ran.

He hung off the side of the horse, the ground pounding away out of control. The horse still screamed. Left foot in a stirrup, Micah clawed at his horse's flank.

The ground struck his head.

4.

Breathe.

Breathe!

Micah inhaled sharp and fast. That's when the pain hit. He was face down on the ground. The dirt was cool against his face. Something rumbled—his horse. It was galloping away. Was he sleeping?

No. He had fallen. His thoughts came to him, gathered them up like a deck of cards that had fallen on the ground. His head hurt, and his left ankle burned. Something crunched inside his mouth. None of that was good. Hopefully the hands would be able to find him after they regathered the herd. He could fire his pistol, of course, if he heard one of them close by. Should be fine.

Roll over. Staring at the dirt isn't going to help you, Micah.

He cried out as he flung himself over onto his back. He lay on a slight incline, his head toward the top of the rise. Above him stars shone bright until a border of darkness cut off their shine. The clouds. They were getting close. And the lightning was close enough now he heard its grumbling over the distant, distant herd.

Cold light flooded the grassland.

A dark shadow drank in the light about a hundred yards away.

The not-quite-a-deer trotted in his direction.

He tried scrambling to his feet, but his head swam, and his ankle gave out. He sprawled on the ground in the darkness. His pistol. He snatched at his belt. His pistol was there. He drew it. He tried drawing it. Something was wrong with his hand. With his arm. He was weak. Couldn't lift the weight of his pistol.

Another flash of light.

It stood in front of him.

It was no deer. Micah didn't know what it was. It was something else. Something older.

He tried to scream, but something in his mouth wouldn't let him.

When the hands found Micah's horse the next dawn, they knew something was wrong. Ben told them that Micah was gone, not worth searching for, but there was a loyalty among the hands. Most of them stayed with the herd and drove them toward Hope River, but a few turned back to find Micah.

They found him just an hour later. At least, they thought it was him. He looked like he'd lain in the sun untouched by predators for weeks. His clothes were tatters, his skin tight and brown against a withered frame. A small tree sprouted out from between his jaws.

On the ground nearby they found deer tracks, but nothing else.

MEAT

1.

Jude swung off his horse and stomped to the big house's stairs. His thick fingers flexed as he walked. His dark, bushy eyebrows drew down. "I thought you said you ain't got no beefs, Jarvis."

The rancher sighed as he came down the stairs. "I don't have any cows for you."

"What about those?" Jude flung a hand at the cows that grazed in the yard. "Look like fine beefs to me. Feed the town just fine. I'll butcher them up good, sell them to Scar Ridge. My money's good. You know it."

Jarvis shook his head. "Those're special to me and the hands."

The butcher spat. "Special? They're beefs. They're for eating. You're getting attached to cows? Think I should tell the parson about it? Ain't natural. And if I don't get some more meat, ain't no one in town gonna be eating any meat for a while. People like that get angry. They need their beefs."

Jarvis's expression didn't change. "I just took a load of cattle to market. Nothing else available for you."

Jude ignored Jarvis's dangerous tone. "Your wife's gonna want some trinkets soon. Women are like that. She'll need some ring or a sweet smelling something-or-other. You ain't gonna find nothing in town for her if you don't let me take them beefs."

Jarvis's face turned thunderous. "I already told you, Jude. Maybe one of the other ranches has something for you."

The butcher ignored him and turned to the nearest cow. She

shied away from his touch. "Look at the brisket on her. She'd be perfect. Just one, Jarvis. Just one, until I can talk to another rancher. You always have the best beefs. Everyone knows it." He crouched and eyed the animal. "I can almost taste her."

Jarvis's fist impacted the side of his face. "You won't talk about Mathilde that way."

Jude shot to his feet and shoved the rancher back. "You're mad!"

"Get off my land before I shoot you."

The butcher took in the pistol Jarvis had already drawn, though it was pointed at the earth. "Jarvis, really? You named a cow? What's wrong with you. You know they're animals. Just meat. That's all they are, and I just want to make sure Scar Ridge has meat."

He jumped as Jarvis shot the ground in front of him.

"Fine. Fine, but don't blame me if people get mad. I'm the butcher. I'm supposed to provide meat, but I can't do that if you don't get me those beefs!" He mounted up and rode back to town, muttering about mad ranchers.

2.

"Ah, Marigold! Flour?" Bart limped from behind the counter to greet the woman.

Marigold offered a shaky smile. "And some sugar too, please."

"Of course." He took her hand and shook it. "Of course! Oh! I'm sorry. I didn't notice. What happened?"

She looked down at her hand. "Just an accident. Nothing serious."

"Nothing serious? That's an entire finger gone from your hand! Is Doc Jasper taking care of you?"

She snatched her hand back. "It's fine. I just need some flour and sugar, please." She lifted her face. "The place is getting fixed up fine, isn't it?"

Bart waved his hand. "Ain't Scar Ridge without Danzig's General Store. We're trying to build back a little bigger. It's gonna take a while to get my Hilda's collection back to what it was before, but that's just fine." He sighed. "You ain't gonna talk more about your hand, are you?"

"I'd rather not, Bart."

"Fine. Fine." He limped back behind the counter to get her flour. "I suppose you got four other fingers. It's still hard to lose something as important as a finger, ain't it?" He groaned as he lifted a sack of flour and set it on the counter. "I should know how hard it is. I'm still not recovered from the fire. Hilda, though, you wouldn't even know there was a fire here at all. You'd think someone that old would have a harder time with something like that."

"That old?"

"Well, she is the woman that raised me!" Bart barked a laugh as he lifted a sack of sugar. "There we go. Anything else, Marigold? Something for your husband, maybe?"

She shook her head. "No. No, Jude's doing just fine. Just the flour and sugar, thank you."

"Tell your husband hello for me."

"Of course, Bart. Thank you."

3.

"You're supposed to be some big hunter. This is all you got?"

Aberdeen looked down. "Two bucks. That's gotta count for something. As much as I usually bring in."

Jude scowled. "Sure. And I'll take them. Jarvis is a stubborn bastard. Won't sell me any beefs. People're gonna be hungry here if I can't get more meat in the store." He crouched and felt along the belly of the nearest buck. "This'll be fine. Any chance you can bring me more?"

The hunter huffed a laugh. "Right. Because the only reason I haven't brought you more is that I didn't feel like it. Look, the herds are thin this year. I've got to go up into the hills, and everything's skittish. Don't know why. Never had this problem until I moved to town."

"Mm." Jude stood. "Well, it's meat. Get me more. Doesn't really matter the kind. Got beaver up there?"

"Beaver?"

"I don't know. What's out there?"

"Coyote. Lizard. Buzzard."

"Bring it all in."

Aberdeen shook his head. "No way. Buzzard ain't good meat. Gets you sick. They eat the dead, and then we eat them? That's not good."

"It's meat, ain't it?"

He frowned. "Something's messed up in you."

Jude's hands curled into fists. "Don't you disrespect me."

"No disrespect." He held up a hand. "Just saying my piece. I'll be back as soon as I got more to sell you. I ain't bringing you buzzard, but I'll see what I can find. Something that's good."

"Just bring me meat. That's good enough."

"Sure, Jude. Sure. Meat."

4.

"You got a new wall, Bart!"

He grinned from behind the counter. "Yep! We raised it yesterday. Should help when winter rolls around. A wall against the wind. How're you doing today, Marigold?"

She stepped forward. "Fine. Just fine. Just stopping by to get some flour."

"Of course. You go through an awful lot."

She shrugged. "It's the way of things. Jude likes pancakes."

"You'd think he'd want more meat, with him being the town butcher and all." Bart groaned as he lifted a bag of flour onto the counter. "He's always been a unique fellow, your husband, long as I've known him. Bit of a temper. A little scary since he handles those knives every day."

"I don't know what you're talking about." She reached for the flour.

Bart pulled the sack away. "What's wrong with your hand?"

"I'm sure I don't know what you're talking about."

"You're missing another finger."

"Mr. Danzig, I'm sure you're just misremembering. I was missing a finger yesterday."

"And now there's another one missing. Another accident?"

She didn't have any expression. "No accident. No more than the last time you saw me. I think perhaps you are getting a bit too personal, sir. Your daughter would not appreciate it."

"Daughter?" He glanced around. "Since when do I have a

daughter?"

Marigold took the opportunity to carry the flour out of the general store, leaving Bart behind.

5.

"Useless. This town's full of useless idiots!" Jude simmered as he sat at the bar. He growled as he lifted the tin mug to his face and sucked down as much beer as he could. Well, it might have been beer. Maybe. Nothing in this town was what it should be. Not the people. Not the beer. Not the meat.

No one answered his complaint. Why would they? This was Sallow. This is where people in Scar Ridge went to bury themselves in sorrow. He was just one more.

Next to him sat Johan, the banker. He liked pretending he didn't come from here. "Not a holy man," he muttered.

On Jude's other side perched one of the hands, probably from Jarvis's farm. "She's a cow," he sobbed.

All of them, idiots.

Idiots who bought his wares. Idiots who were content whatever the meat was. They didn't ask. He didn't tell. He'd rather have beef. He'd rather have venison. There just wasn't enough, though. There was never going to be enough.

He could always take a cleaver to one of the people here. No one would notice. Enough people went missing. Sheriff Carter never found them. He eyed the hand. They ride off to other ranches often enough.

"Don't do it."

He turned to the bartender. "Do what?"

The man in the dark vest shrugged. "What you're thinking. Not worth it."

"I don't know what you're talking about." He tipped the mug to his face again.

"You stopped complaining. You looked at Harald here. I know exactly what you were thinking." He snatched the mug from Jude and filled it before handing it back. "I've served enough people here."

Jude glared. "I'm an honorable man."

"Course you are."

"I'd never kill someone. Not for their meat."

"Good to know." The bartender nodded.

"If they said I wasn't good enough. Or if they kept me from doing my job. But not for their meat."

"Since you're honorable."

"Exactly."

The bartender moved away, poured a few more drinks, and returned. "So why are people idiots?"

"Because they want meat, but I can't get enough."

"You had enough earlier today when I stopped by."

"I shouldn't have." He turned his glare to his mug.

"What do you mean?"

"I ran out yesterday. Didn't have anything left. Came in this morning. Plenty there. Enough to last the day." He narrowed his eyes. "I don't know where the meat's coming from, and that scares me. What am I feeding people?"

6.

When Marigold came to Danzig's, Bart didn't say a word to her. He lifted her sack of flour and took her payment. He watched her hand, though.

She only had two fingers left on it.

His heart squeezed. He should say something. He should do something. But what? What if it was just an accident?

No. Doc Jasper talked too much. He would've said something if she'd lost that many fingers in just a week. The whole town would be whispering. This wasn't an accident, though.

And that meant someone did it to her. Someone she didn't want to talk about.

What a man did with his woman behind closed doors, that was his business. His and hers. But that kind of violence? Chopping off fingers? She didn't say anything because she was scared. Of course she was. Jude wasn't a little man. He had a temper. Everyone knew.

Bart kept chewing the thought as people came and went. More flour. Lard. Nails. He sold it all. No one asked for his collection, which was fine. It wasn't even his collection. It was Hilda's. Right now he wished he knew enough about her collection, though. She had things there that might help.

But no. He was just a man.

And sometimes a man had to stand up to another man to protect a woman.

7.

Jude kept his home just a little out of town. Bart limped out the entire way. By the time he made it to the place, his hip burned and he was gasping for breath.

Big man, gonna go protect a helpless woman. Right. He didn't even really know how to use the pistol at his side. He knew how to point and shoot, but that wasn't enough, and he knew it. Maybe he should have talked to Sheriff Carter first.

No. No, he had to do this. He didn't really know anything. Marigold just needed someone to step in. Maybe.

Bart leaned against one of the posts on the low porch outside the house and tried to get his breathing under control. If he banged on the door gasping like this, they'd probably figure he was here to rob the place. After a few moments he thought he might be able to fake he was fine. He limped the last few feet and banged on the door.

Jude answered a moment later. He stood in a dirty white shirt, his eyes bloodshot. "What?" he barked.

"Jude."

"Bart."

"Can I come in?"

"I don't think so." He stank of whiskey.

"How're things with you and Marigold?"

Jude narrowed his eyes. "Not a thing you should be asking her husband."

"Maybe not. But she's not been good lately."

"What're you saying?" He drew himself as tall as he could, which was plenty tall. He towered over Bart.

Bart tried answering, but his hip chose that moment to give out and he fell against the wall. His shoulder banged against the wood. He yelped in pain. After a gasp, he answered, "I ain't saying anything, Jude, except she's been pretty banged up. And you've got a little bit of a temper."

"You think I'd lay a hand on my wife?" His hands curled into fists. "You accusing me of that?"

Bart forced himself back to his feet. "She's been missing fingers. You taking your cleaver to her hand?"

"What?" Jude blinked. "Missing fingers?"

Bart opened his mouth, then closed it. "You didn't notice?"

"We don't talk much. Ever since she joined that women's group at the chapel."

"Women's group?" He frowned.

"She says she meets at the chapel. Something going on there every night lately. Maybe she's just praying. I've been... well, I've been busy at the butcher."

Bart shook his head. "Pretty sure there ain't no women's group."

"So where is she?"

"Maybe we should see what she's been doing at the chapel."

8.

Thankfully Jude let Bart ride behind him. His hip wasn't going to take another trip. Ever since the shop burned down, he hadn't been able to walk well. They rode out to the chapel. Though the half-moon lit the sky, there were no lights shining from within the chapel.

Jude growled, "Where is that woman?"

Bart shushed him. "Do you hear that?"

They paused. The horse stood still. Some sound floated to them in the night air.

"What is that?" Bart asked.

"It's meat." Jude slipped off the horse. "It's the sound of meat slapping a smooth floor after it's been cut off a carcass." He moved to sneak past the corner of the chapel.

Bart got himself off the horse and followed. "That's probably not a good sound."

Jude didn't answer. Instead, he grunted. "Chapel always had a cellar?"

"No idea. My woman doesn't like me going to chapel."

"I don't go either. Not normally. But I didn't think anyone had cellars here." Jude stabbed a finger toward a low door in the ground near the base of the building. It was open, revealing a dark stone step. A distant flickering light beckoned from below. Another sound of flesh slapping pavement echoed from the hole. Jude stepped to the door.

Bart limped after. He put his hand on the pistol's grip. It wouldn't really do anything, but it still made him feel better. They walked down the stone steps together.

The air turned warm. It smelled of rot. It felt like flies were crawling over his skin, but he didn't hear any of the buzzing. Down, down they went.

"This ain't no cellar," Jude breathed.

Bart didn't answer.

Up ahead, they heard a voice, cold, feminine. "Flesh for flesh!"

Something like the sound of meat slapping against meat answered. No, that wasn't right. It was bigger than meat. Like someone took the carcass of a bull and slammed it against the carcass of a whale, thick and wet.

The two men glanced at each other. Jude's face was pale. He pressed his lips together and pushed farther down the staircase. The air turned warmer, like the inside of a cow that had just been slaughtered.

The voice continued, "I give of my flesh. Give of yours!"

Now the sound of a heavy corpse dragging across the ground. Chunks of flesh tore from it.

The light brightened. Ahead the steps turned.

"To save my husband, I choose to give of myself." And then the voice cried out in pain.

It was like a thousand dead pigs rotted as one, releasing the sound of a forest of meat collapsing in on itself.

They reached the turn. Jude stepped around it, his fists clenched. He screamed and collapsed, gibbering and pointing at what he saw.

Bart steeled himself. He drew his pistol. Whatever was there, he had to face it. If Marigold was there. If Jude wasn't man enough to handle it, he had to be.

And then Marigold rushed to her husband's side. "Jude! What're you doing here?" She held a knife in one hand. Her other hand flowed with blood, another finger gone.

"Marigold," Bart croaked. He didn't have to turn the corner.

He didn't have to see whatever was there, whatever she had been talking to. "We have to go. Come on."

"No. I need to finish here. Take Jude back. He'll have his meat. Tell him I'll be home soon."

"But—"

She smiled up at him. "I'll be home soon. He'll have his meat."

Bart turned his back to whatever was beyond the corner. It smelled of blood and flesh. The feeling of flies on his skin grew a thousandfold. He hauled Jude up as best he could and began dragging him up, up, up. Behind him, Marigold's voice continued. The sound of meat and decomposition continued.

And the next day, Jude had more meat to sell.

THE STORY OF SOME NAUGHTY CHILDREN

1.

"**N**aughty books get put in the fire." Ms. Kettering snatched the book from Thomas Anderson's hands. "You should know better than to bring these nasty books into my classroom."

"But Ms. Kettering!"

She glared at him. "Mr. Anderson, I believe you are familiar with the dunce stool."

His lips trembled.

She waved the book. "These terrible pulp books that you get from Mr. Danzig's store are worthless. Worse than worthless. They put terrible ideas in your head about what men and women do. They're lurid, they're vile, and they use terrible grammar. You will not bring such trash into this classroom again." She marched to the stove at the front of the little one-room schoolhouse and opened the grate. Inside, logs sputtered and coals glowed. "Mr. Anderson. This is all your book is good for." She threw *Walking the Plank* into the stove.

The pages blackened and curled. The cover illustration faded to ash.

Thomas wouldn't let himself cry. He'd saved up to buy that. He thought Ms. Kettering would be proud of him. Actually reading!

But nothing was good enough for the old witch. Not if he was going to do it. He was just a naughty boy and that's all he'd ever be to her. He felt a great heat in his chest. He was going to shout at her, wasn't he? He wasn't supposed to do that. His papa always beat him when he shouted like that.

"Mr. Anderson. I believe I told you to sit on the dunce stool."

"Yes, Ms. Kettering." He dragged himself to his feet. He wanted to shout. He wanted to throw his primer at her. He wanted to run away and never come back. Instead, he trudged up the narrow passage between desks and took his position at the front of the classroom.

The teacher turned to the other students. "Now, boys and girls, we will be practicing our letters. Take out your slates, please. Youngers, you'll be practicing the letter F. Olders, you will teach and correct as needed. Beatrice, you will come forward for private instruction."

The other children turned to their tasks. Thomas risked a look over his shoulder.

Jenny Collins glanced up at him. She looked sad. Then she ducked her head and helped Conner Friedholm make an F on his slate.

Thomas thought about that burning book. It was going to be a good book. Pirates and heroes and lots of swordfights. Ms. Kettering didn't want him to read. She thought he was a naughty boy.

Well, if she thought he was naughty, he might as well be naughty. He'd get her back.

2.

Somewhere a horse nickered. The dirt skritched under Thomas's boots. He tried to walk slower. He couldn't wake Ms. Kettering up, and her ears were so sharp she could hear him whisper to Jenny Collins. Ain't no one could hear that well. Maybe she was a witch.

The night air chilled him as he crouched behind a low barrel cactus. Well, he tried to. His mama said he ate too much, but he was just hungry. He was a growing boy! And he couldn't hide behind no barrel cactuses anymore unless they were really big, and this one wasn't.

He wished the buildings in town here were closer together. Ms. Kettering lived in that house. All he had to do was sneak in and not wake her up, and he'd pull the best trick on her. Get her back for burning his book.

He checked for the thousandth time. Yep. The glass jar was still there, and still full of all the scorpions he could catch this afternoon after school let out and before Ma could make him do chores.

Perfect. Most of them were still scurrying around in there.

No lights on in the house. She must be asleep. It was after midnight. No good boys or girls were up this late. His parents were snoring when he snuck out of the house. He wondered if maybe Ms. Kettering snored.

He snorted a laugh, and then ducked as low as he could. Still, nothing moved. No terrible teacher stormed from the house. No crack opened in the ground to swallow him whole.

He grinned. He was going to get away with this, wasn't he?

Thomas crouched and tiptoed toward the house, one quiet skritch at a time. His heart pounded pretty loud, but only he could hear that. If anyone could, he would've woken his ma up a hundred times for as often as he snuck out to catch bugs or try to sneak into Candide.

Somehow, he always got caught there. He just wanted to see the girls that his older brother said were there! Thankfully no one ever told his parents about it, though. Good thing. He couldn't handle the paddling they'd give him.

That horse nickered again, wherever it was. He froze.

No lanterns lit. No terrible faces appeared in any window.

Good. He stepped forward again, again, again—he was at a low window. It was cracked open to let in the cool night air. It was pretty good for letting in naughty little boys, too. He scurried in as quick and as silent as could be.

No snoring inside that he could hear. The three-quarters moon lit up the room pretty good. A counter. A breadbox. A table and two chairs. A stove that still held some orange coals. Pitcher and basin. A door that led to another room—probably her bedroom. He didn't need to go in there, though. The scorpions weren't for her bed. He was naughty, sure, but he wasn't that mean.

He shuffled toward the counter. There were jars marked for flour, for sugar, other little dishes for whatever moms used to make food.

His steps didn't skritch anymore. Now they sort of whumphed. He did his best to walk silent. Quiet feet!

No one jumped out of the bedroom with a rifle. No one demanded that he sit in the corner. No one marched him to Sheriff Carter's office for being a bad boy.

He finally spotted the tin can he wanted. Coffee. Perfect. As quiet as could be, he opened his glass jar and slid the scorpions into the coffee grounds. Let her find *those* in the morning! He should be able to hear the scream from his bedroom. He held back a snicker.

He'd done it. All he had to do was sneak out now. Simple again! He turned to whumph his way back to the window.

Something on the table caught his eye. Was that a pad of paper? He frowned. Why would Ms. Kettering leave that on her table? The moon was so bright, he might even be able to read it. He snuck his way to the table, just a few steps aside from where he'd been going. He recognized Ms. Kettering's perfect handwriting. Ain't no one wrote as pretty as her, not any of the girls, not even Jenny Collins, and definitely not any of the boys.

He glanced at the writing. Should he steal it?

Nah. He already had his revenge. He was about to turn away when he spotted his name on the page. He frowned. What was going on? He read:

Somewhere a horse nickered. The dirt skritched under Thomas's boots. He tried to walk slower. He couldn't wake Ms. Kettering up, and her ears were so sharp she could hear him whisper to Jenny Collins. Ain't no one could hear that well. Maybe she was a witch.

He gasped.

3.

Jenny Collins followed the other children into the classroom. Ms. Kettering sat at her desk, sipping coffee and reading some book. The coals in the stove glowed warmth. Jenny took her seat and looked around.

Where was Thomas?

The coals in the oven popped. Jenny glanced, and then looked closer. That looked like another book burning in there. Why would Ms. Kettering start a fire with a book? It didn't make any sense. She always wanted the children to be reading. It had been a crime what she did to Thomas yesterday. If it had been any of the other children, Jenny would think that Thomas just decided not to come to school, but his parents were strict. He didn't miss any day that school was in session.

"You know where Thomas is?" she asked Paul, one of Thomas's friends.

He shrugged. "Don't know. Probably run away."

"That ain't like Thomas," she said.

"His parents were looking for him this morning." Paul glanced up at the teacher. "You think maybe she did something?"

"She's mean, but she wouldn't do something like that!"

"Class!" Ms. Kettering stood. "Quiet please. It is time to begin the day." She tore some paper out of the book she'd been reading and tossed it in the fire. She held her hand out, absorbing some of the heat. "Friendship provides a certain warmth, don't you think?"

Jenny craned her neck. "What'd you throw in the fire, Ms. Kettering?"

"Oh, that? Just something I wrote. I like writing at night. Not naughty stories, of course. I write about good boys and girls." She smiled sweetly. "Stories about how nice they are, about how kind they are to each other, how they obey all the time. But sometimes I don't like what I write. When that happens, I just throw the story into the fire. Then it doesn't bother me anymore." She gazed at the coals.

Jenny got a bad feeling in her stomach. "You always like writing, Ms. Kettering?"

"Oh, this is something new. Hilda and Danzig's had some papers I bought. Ever since then, I've been writing such good stories. Maybe the stories are so good they scare away naughty boys like Thomas."

"Shit!" Paul swore.

Ms. Kettering spun around. "Mr. Newsome! None of that now! Swearing is so naughty!"

4.

The next day Paul was gone.

"He must be with Thomas," Ms. Kettering said. "Their friendship is keeping them warm. Paul and Thomas were always such naughty boys. Always late. Not like you, Jenny. You've always been such a good girl, haven't you?"

More papers burned in the fire.

"Ms. Kettering, may I go find them? Please?" Jenny asked.

"Oh, no. A good girl like you wouldn't like to find them. They only caused disruptions in this classroom. All of you will learn so much better without them. Now, take out your slates."

5.

Jenny huddled behind the barrel cactus. It was the only thing to hide behind, really. It's not like any trees grew in the town. Just a few cactuses here and there. And this one wasn't far from Ms. Kettering's window.

Inside, the teacher scratched at some papers with a pencil. Her tongue poked out of one corner of her mouth. She'd call that naughty if Jenny did it in the classroom, but apparently it wasn't naughty if she did it at home.

Jenny shook her head. Ms. Kettering was just like all the other adults, talking about behaving so good but never doing it themselves. Just like how her mom always told Jenny to be nice, but was never nice at home. Just another adult that liked pretending.

The teacher sat back with a sigh and looked down at her papers. She gave a sharp nod and stood. With another sigh, she took up her lantern and left the room. A door inside closed.

Jenny waited. Mom wouldn't notice she was gone for a few hours yet. She was busy at Candide trying to get some money. Dad was on the trail again. Probably wouldn't be back for another month.

Ms. Kettering said she was a good little girl. Jenny wasn't, though. Why would she be good when none of the adults were good?

Something screeched in the night. Probably an owl. It didn't bother Jenny any. She'd seen plenty of owls sitting on her roof. She kept crouching behind the barrel cactus. How long would it take Ms. Kettering to fall asleep?

Why was she even doing this? It was one thing to sneak out at night. It was another thing to sneak into her teacher's house.

But the teacher knew something about Thomas and Paul. She was too happy about them being gone. She didn't know what the teacher did, but she must have done something. Of course she had. She was evil with a smile, the worst kind of evil.

Jenny waited another while, breathing slowly, before sneaking to the half-open window. As quiet as she was when she snuck out of her house, she snuck just as quiet into Ms. Kettering's house. On silent feet she crept around. Had she killed them and used them for stew meat? Had she turned them into frogs? Or maybe she just plucked out their hairs, and with every hair they turned a year older, until they were only dust.

No. All that was silly. People didn't do things like that. They were evil, not magic.

So what should she do? Look around, sure. Stay out here in the kitchen. Don't go into the bedroom. She could sneak, but not that good. Probably. Not unless Ms. Kettering was drunk, but she didn't think the teacher could get drunk, since she didn't drink any. She called alcohol a terrible evil, after all.

Or was that just another smiling lie?

Didn't matter. She hadn't seen her drinking anything, so she wasn't going to risk going into the bedroom. There wasn't much to look at here, though.

Nothing except whatever Ms. Kettering had been writing. Stories about good boys and girls? Jenny crept to the table. By the light of the almost-full moon, she read:

Jenny huddled behind the barrel cactus. It was the only thing to hide behind, really. It's not like any trees grew in the town. Just a few cactuses here and there. And this one wasn't far from Ms. Kettering's window.

She gasped. Ms. Kettering was writing about her? And here she wasn't being a good girl. How could the teacher know? Did she have a look outside and see her? Jenny kept reading. It was like she couldn't move. She read how she snuck into the house. She read how she was reading the story. And then she went home. In the morning, Ms. Kettering burned the story about the naughty little girl named Jenny, and Jenny herself turned to ash and blew away in the wind.

And that's where Ms. Kettering's beautiful handwriting ended.

6.

Jenny came to school early the next morning. Ms. Kettering was just getting the fire going in the stove. "Oh, Jenny!" she said as she saw the girl. "I suppose you would come early today. You have always been such a naughty girl, haven't you? Sneaking around. I would expect nothing else from what your mama does when your papa's away."

Jenny felt her ears burn. "You're naughty," she whispered back. It's not like it mattered what she said now, did it? She'd awakened that morning and come early. She couldn't stop herself. It was like Ms. Kettering's story had taken over her life, and now she'd have to watch as her story burned.

"Oh, and I suppose you would say that. Naughty children often accuse good adults of that."

"Isn't it naughty to want to hurt someone?"

"Judges want to hurt criminals, and they're not naughty. They're simply doing justice on the land." The teacher stirred up the coals.

"Unless the judge is wrong."

"Miss Collins! I will not accept such statements in my classroom! This is a good place. A proper place! There's no place for naughty children here." She strode to her desk and plucked up a few sheets of paper. Nice, clean handwriting covered them. "And you already know that. That's why you're here. The same reason Paul was here yesterday, and Thomas the day before that. So my stories have a happy ending with no more naughty children!"

Jenny braced herself. She couldn't run. Her legs wouldn't listen.

The teacher threw the papers into the fire. They blackened. They curled. Flames ate them. Ms. Kettering spun and grinned at Jenny.

Jenny didn't turn to ash.

Ms. Kettering frowned. "Now, you are a naughty girl, aren't you? You're breaking the rules of how the story's supposed to go." She shook a finger at Jenny.

Her finger turned black and curled.

Ms. Kettering's eyes popped so wide, Jenny thought her face might turn inside out. "What have you done?" the teacher whispered. Her hand shriveled up.

"I wrote a story last night," Jenny answered, a smile growing on her face as the black spread up Ms. Kettering's arm. "A story about a naughty, naughty teacher. I left it on your table. I practiced my best handwriting for it, too. Didn't you read it?"

"Jenny, you are a naughty, naughty girl." Her voice scratched and burned. Her dress smoldered. Her blackened arm fell off her shoulder and burst into ash as it struck the floor. She stumbled forward. "And naughty girls will be punished!"

Jenny stood her ground. "You can't punish me!"

Ms. Kettering raised her remaining hand, ready to strike her. She stepped forward. Her blackening leg buckled and collapsed. She tumbled to the floor. Her body burst into a thousand thousand flakes of ash and fluttered around the classroom. Her head rolled forward and glared at Jenny. "Naughty!" she bellowed.

Jenny shrugged. "I guess I am." She raised a foot. "Nice girls don't get to kill witches like you." She stomped down.

The teacher's head shattered to ash.

HOME AGAIN

1.

David's mama glowed. "Oh, you look like such a fine young man." She tugged on the blue coat. "Just imagine, everyone waving flags and you coming right down Main Street. They want to throw you a parade, you know. Oh, I'm so proud of you!"

David shook his head. "No. No, Mama. I just got home." His fingers twitched. Yeah. Just imagine it. All those people watching him. All those people cheering.

They shouldn't cheer.

"Mama, I just want to rest. Just for a little bit. I don't need no parade. I didn't do nothing worthy of a parade."

"Oh, you hush now! You're a soldier. You survived our little war. Kept the Union. You deserve the respect of our town. Imagine that, the only person brave enough to go and fight for us. But it's over now. You deserve a celebration! You're home. You're safe."

David frowned. No. He wasn't safe. And yes, he was home, but not for long. He'd have to go, and go soon. At least there weren't any trees here. Just a horizon that ended in distant mountains. He'd know if anyone was following soon enough.

"I can tell them to wait on the parade if you want, I suppose." Mama pressed her lips together, her eyes glassy. "But everyone's so happy you're back, David. Everyone."

Everyone? "Whatever happened to Maggie Clair?"

The older woman turned away. "Oh. Well, you leave her be. I

know you were sweet on her years ago, but she works at Candide now. One of *those* women. An honorable soldier like you wouldn't want to spend time with a woman like her."

"Candide?"

"Forget I said anything. And forget about her." She nodded for emphasis. "She's gone and ruined her life, and you've gone and made something out of yours."

He reached up to unbutton the jacket.

"Oh, why are you taking it off?"

"I'm not a soldier anymore, Mama. I'm out." His fingers shook a little. He forced them to obey. "I shouldn't be in uniform at all. I only put it on because you told me to."

"And I only told you to because—"

"Because you're proud of me. I know." He finally pried the last button undone and took the coat off. "But it's hot. And I'm not a soldier." And I don't want to think about what I did while I wore that coat.

"Well, if you're going to be that way." She flung her hands up. "Go ahead, I suppose. But I know the truth, David. I know who you really are. A soldier I am proud of. My son, a man who fought for his country, a man who would make his father proud if he were still alive."

David nodded, even though he knew otherwise. No, Dad wouldn't be proud. No one would be proud. No, he was just here to say goodbye and move on before the hunters caught up to him.

2.

Darkness covered most of Main Street. It hadn't changed much since the last time he'd been here. Danzig's looked bigger and newer, but the blacksmith and the schoolhouse seemed the same. Before he left, he'd never touched liquor. His parents had been very firm about that. Now, though...

Well, he had two choices. That hadn't changed either. There was Sallow, for when you thought the world was over, and there was Candide, for when you wanted to celebrate.

The world was over, for him at least. Nothing left but to say goodbye. Sallow was where he belonged.

But Candide. Light fairly exploded from the bright windows. Out here he heard gay singing. A piano jangled. People laughed.

He didn't belong there. Not one bit of him belonged there. There was nothing to celebrate in what he'd done. Nothing good that anyone should be happy to see him.

But Maggie was in Candide, wasn't she?

That made up his mind for him. He strode toward the swinging doors and stepped in.

Merriment slapped him in the face. The air itself felt joyous. He smiled despite himself. A polished bar filled one entire side of the room. Glass bottles nearly overflowing with every color of liquid lined the shelves behind the bar. Women wearing scandalous clothing poured glasses back there. On the far side of the room, a man pounded at a piano. More than a few patrons sang along. Some danced. Tables filled most of the rest of the space, and many of them were occupied by men. A grand staircase led to a balcony. More scandalous women stood atop the balcony, beckoning the men below.

And there was Maggie. Brown hair. Brown eyes. A perfect little nose. He'd recognize her any day, even though he hadn't seen her in years. 'Course, last time he'd seen her, he hadn't been seeing so much of her. He gulped. There was a lot of her to see, and he instantly felt dirty that he could see so much, and then he felt guilty that maybe he didn't feel guilty enough, and then he felt guilty that he was still staring at her.

His fingers twitched. He probably shouldn't be standing in the door like that. He should get a drink. He had some money from when he mustered out. He could get a drink. Yeah. He just had to stop staring at Maggie.

But just look at her.

How many men had looked at her that way? How many men had visited her? How many men had seen even more of her?

He laughed at himself. It didn't matter. She was Maggie. She was the only other person besides Mama that he'd come back for. And if she worked here, maybe that would make her happy. Maybe she'd find some man to take her away. That'd be better for her.

She saw him. She saw him laugh. Something changed in her eyes. He could tell even from this distance. He'd done something wrong. He was always doing something wrong.

He finally shook himself and moved to the bar. A man with a magnificent handlebar mustache greeted him. "Why, it's David! I ain't never seen you in here before, sir! First drink's free, in honor of your coming home."

He lifted a hand. "I can pay."

"Course you can! And you will for the second drink!" The bartender barked a rich laugh. "What'll it be?"

"We didn't get much but beer in the Army."

"So you want beer, or something a touch finer?"

He looked up at all those bottles and all their colors. "No. I don't need anything finer. Just give me a beer."

"Whatever you say, son. It's my pleasure." He snatched a mug up from behind the bar and filled it, dropping a sudsy glass in front of David. "Drink up, drink hearty, and feel free to visit the rooms upstairs! I saw you staring. I suppose you know all about that, a military man and all!" He guffawed.

"No." David felt his ears burn. "Not really."

"Well, maybe it's about time you learned, then." The bartender winked. "I suppose we've never met properly. Major Ellis." He offered a meaty hand.

"David Frelitz."

"A pleasure." They shook. "And I see you caught someone's eye." He winked again and moved away to take care of another patron.

David turned and nearly jumped out of his skin. Maggie stood beside him. "Hi," she said.

He stammered. His hands shook. Finally, he squeezed out, "Hi."

"I saw you at the door. You're home."

He forced himself to look only at her face. Oh, he was so dirty, wasn't he? She was so pretty and so... well, lots of things. "Yes," he finally stuttered. "I'm home. And I saw Mama. And I see you." Of course he saw her. She was standing right there. All of her was standing right there, in fact.

"Davey. I'm glad you're home."

His ears burned even more. His head was going to explode. "Yes! And you're home. I mean, you're here. At my house. No." He squeezed his eyes shut. "Mama said you'd be here."

When he opened his eyes, Maggie's face had darkened. "Your mama don't approve."

"No."

"Course she don't. But this is what I do now." She spat every word.

"Yes! And you're... Um... You're good at it."

She slapped him. "David Frelitz, if you came in here to make fun of me, that I'm not good enough for you, you turn around and go home. I don't need your pity!" She spun to stalk away.

"No!" He licked his lips. "No! You're just... You deserve so much better than anything I could give. And there's something out there, Mags. I just had to see you again. Before... Well." He gave a half-smile as she turned back to him. "Something's out there."

"Course there is, Davey. Well, ain't nothing here free. You want to talk, you can spend coin, like any other man."

His stomach dropped. He nodded.

She stalked back up the stairs and disappeared into the upstairs.

"Every soldier feels guilty, son." Major Ellis was on the other side of the bar again. "Every single one. If they don't, they're monsters."

"Some of us are monsters," David answered.

3.

David sat at the kitchen table and chopped potatoes. Mama kneaded dough. "Well, if we can't have a parade, we'll have to have a welcome luncheon at the chapel. I'll talk to Parson Dies."

"Parson Dies?"

"Our new parson. Came in not quite half a year ago. He don't talk much, but he's a good man, pretty sure. I hope so, anyway."

"I don't need a luncheon, Mama."

"Nonsense! Why don't you let people treat you like the hero you are?" She slapped the dough onto the table and worked it as if it might be someone's face she disliked. "You're a good boy. You've always been a good boy. And good boys should be rewarded."

David leaned back in the chair. "What if they're not really

good boys?"

Mama stood up straight. "You don't talk that way. You've never talked that way before."

"War changes a person, Mama."

"Course it does. I seen enough of that in my life. You're not the first soldier I've loved, David. Not the first man who came back thinking they weren't nothing. But you know what? Every single one of them was wrong. They were all heroes. Anyone who came back is a hero, and you came back." She smiled kindly. "You came back to me. And you're worthy of celebration."

He got up and paced away. "You don't know, Mama."

"Nope. And I don't have to. I know you. That's enough. Now get back over here and chop those potatoes."

He turned back. "Or what?"

"Or you don't get your biscuits. I know you well enough to know that you need those biscuits, or you'll keel over with your hands on your stomach, crying about how terrible this world is."

He chuckled despite himself. "Only if they got butter."

"What do you take me for? Of course they'll have butter!"

He took his place again. "Well, for butter, I suppose I could chop potatoes."

4.

Maggie's mama didn't like her much. She wasn't afraid to tell her. She'd cover her face. "Oh, what the ladies say to me at chapel!" she'd declare.

She never argued when Maggie paid the rent, though.

A man lay snoring in Maggie's bed at Candide. She pulled the plain dress over her head. No one ever claimed to recognize her when she went out dressed like any other woman. When she was working, no one stared at her face. Right now, she just wanted to walk home to her mama. Maybe get some fresh bread if her mama wasn't too drunk.

Not that any ladies at the chapel ever heard about how much mama drank, just about what Maggie did to get some coin. Now how would the ladies know about Maggie but not her mama?

It didn't matter. None of it mattered. She made a living, and that was enough. It's all she needed.

She clomped down the back stairs into the night. She inhaled the dusty air. It was good to get out of that humid building. It always smelled like... like happiness bought at a price. The air out here was honest, though. Dry and brittle and harsh all at once.

The half-moon shed some illumination on the desert around the town. Plenty of low weeds. A few saguaros. The shadows of mountains in the distance. A place more honest than almost anyone who lived here. Especially the men.

She scowled. Why did Davey come home? Why did he have to come and see her? She almost couldn't work the rest of her shift, he got her so worked up. And acting like what she was doing was shameful.

It didn't matter, she told herself. Of course it didn't matter. Just one more man judging while still staring at her.

Maggie set out toward the other leg of the town's T, heading toward her mama's house. It was late, but she'd probably be up if she wasn't passed out from drink. Either way, her house smelled better than her room at the bar.

She lifted her head up. At least she had a place to go. Most of the girls had to stay at Candide every night.

She almost ran into the tree. She blinked. What was a tree doing here? There weren't any trees in town. Some out by the ranches, sure, but here? She'd never noticed it before. Look at that. It was a big one, too.

And it smelled *green*. She couldn't find any other words to describe it. Like a thousand shades of green in the darkness. There wasn't a single leaf on the ground. There weren't any other trees she could see. Just one tree, thicker around than her hips, stretching up toward the sky. Its branches obscured the moon.

What was a tree doing here?

She exhaled. Was this some sort of trick? Did someone plant a tree during the day? It didn't make any sense. She reached out and placed her palm against the rough bark.

She should show someone. But who? Major would still be running things at the bar until dawn. Most of the girls were on shift. If Mama was awake, she'd just yell at Maggie's foolishness.

Davey would like it.

She shook her head. No, Davey wouldn't like it. He would just... she didn't know what she'd do. It didn't matter what Davey thought.

Well. There was a tree here. So that was good. It would still be here in the morning. She set out for Mama's house, hoping for bread.

When she returned in the morning, there was no tree.

5.

"Gotta pay today, son," Major Ellis said as David took a seat.

He placed a nickel on the bar.

The bartender nodded and poured a mug. "Looking for anyone in particular?" he asked.

David shrugged, but his ears burned.

"I thought as much. She'll be out in just a little bit." Major nodded toward the balcony.

Several women stood there already, winking at the men in the room. Most of the men had come in for lunch. They weren't interested in the ladies' services yet, but it was always good to have something pretty to look at. As David looked up, Maggie took her spot. It might have been the same dress, showing so much of her off.

She immediately spotted David. Her cheeks turned pink. She stepped around the other girls and made her way down the stairs. Soon enough she perched on the stool next to him. "So I guess seeing you did something to me," she said.

He held up a hand. "I, um, I wanted to say I'm sorry. Because. Well. I didn't want to embarrass you. I just wanted to see you again." Why were his ears so hot?

She gave a little nod. "Yeah. I'm a little sensitive. Most of the women in town don't treat us too good, you know?" Her voice was low.

"And those women just don't know how to have a good time," guffawed Major as he set a shot glass in front of Maggie. He shrugged at her glare and moved off to chat with another patron.

Maggie ignored the glass. "How are you, Davey?"

He shrugged. "I'm fine. Not going to be in town long. Just wanted to see, well, I wanted to see you again." He kept his eyes on her face. "Like I said. Because. Well."

She nodded. "Yeah. We were real close once, weren't we?"

He didn't think his ears could burn any hotter without lighting the place on fire.

She refused to look away from him. "Remember how we used to talk about moving away? Going someplace where there were forests? I guess seeing you reminded me. Last night when I was walking home, I thought I saw a tree."

David stiffened.

She sighed a little laugh. "It felt green. It didn't belong here at all. I must have been dreaming, though. No trees this morning!"

David stood. "I need to go."

"What's wrong, Davey?"

"I need to go." He stumbled out of Candide, his beer untouched. Maggie watched him go with a sad, sad look.

6.

David stayed at home for the next week. He shook as he stared out the window. His fingers never stopped twitching. Every time his mama opened the door, he flinched. He was going mad, but he couldn't get himself to move. He had to do something. Anything.

Finally, finally one morning he stepped outside and scanned the horizon. Dust. Dirt. Some cactuses. The mountains in the distance.

No trees. Not a single tree.

Well, there was nothing to be scared of then, was there? Maggie must have been seeing things. Who knows how wrong in the head she was now.

He instantly felt guilty for the thought. Maggie wasn't being moral, no, but it was her life. He hadn't been part of it for years. He shouldn't have expected her to wait for him. He shouldn't be judging her. He wasn't Mama. He wasn't some old lady that thought they knew better.

And he was worse than anything she could have ever been.

Scar Ridge wasn't that bad, was it? He'd be able to see anything sneaking up on him. And how could anything find him here? He was so far away. Maybe he could stay. He'd been here over a week now, and nothing bad had happened. He could stay with Mama. Take care of her, like she should be taken care of.

Maybe see Maggie again.

He took a deep breath. If he was going to stay, he needed to find something to do. He had to stay busy. He'd been a soldier. He'd followed orders like a good soldier. All he had to do was figure out someone that would give him orders and pay him for following. He could sign on at one of the ranches, but there were trees out there. He'd never be able to relax. His fingers twitched just thinking about that.

So not out there. Something in town. Major didn't need any help at Candide. He'd probably be too distracted by Maggie to work there anyway. Mr. Danzig probably didn't need any help. The butcher was out, too. He didn't want to work with meat. It would remind him too much of the battlefield. Mr. Schmidt wouldn't take him on at the bank. He didn't know numbers that well.

He was quickly running out of businesses.

What about the blacksmith? He could handle a hammer. He knew horses well enough to shoe them. He could pound out nails.

He nodded. The blacksmith. What was the smithy's name? Ezra. That was it.

David took a deep, deep breath. He could leave the house. No leaves here. No branches holding back the sky. Just a distant horizon. He was safe.

Another breath, and he set off, the dirt skritching under his boots. He turned down Main Street until he found the building marked BLACKSMITH. He wandered into the yard to see a large, hairy man pumping a bellows.

"Be with you in a moment," he roared over the sound of the fire he pumped. Finally, he let go of the bellows, grabbed some tongs, and pulled a glowing piece of metal from the fire. He set it on a nearby anvil and pounded it once, twice, three times. Sparks scattered. He lifted the dimming metal and regarded it. With a nod he slipped it into a bucket of water. Steam exploded.

Finally, the man turned to him. "Yeah?"

"Mr. Ezra?" David asked.

"Ezra will do."

"Right. Ezra. I'm David Frelitz. I just got back to town. I'm looking for a job."

The blacksmith nodded.

"So. Do you have anything I can do?"

Ezra grunted and motioned to the bellows. "Pump that."

He considered the bellows. Well, he could handle that. Sure. He stepped up and put his hands on the handles. They were warm enough they almost burned his hands. Here next to the furnace the air stung his face. Sweat broke out all over his body. He began pumping.

Ezra turned and took a chunk of metal with his tongs before placing it in the fire. After a moment he placed a second, and then a third. He didn't say anything.

So David didn't say anything. He simply pumped.

Ezra watched the fire. After a while, he retrieved the first chunk, pounded it, slipped it back into the furnace. Then he worked the second, then the third, and on in rotation. After a while he'd pounded out several nails and cooled them. Then he started the process over again.

And David pumped. He set up a rhythm. Inhale. Exhale. Inhale. It was as mindless as marching. He slipped into that haze of not having to do anything but exist.

"Day's done." Ezra took off the thick gloves he'd been wearing. "Come back tomorrow."

David blinked. The sun hung low in the sky. "Oh. Is that it?"

"No. Enough for now. Come back tomorrow."

He nodded. "Thank you, Mr. Ezra. Ezra! Sorry. I'll see you tomorrow. In the morning?"

The blacksmith nodded.

Well, at least he had a job now.

7.

"Lunch time." Ezra slipped off his gloves.

"I'll be back," David answered, wiping sweat from his face.

The blacksmith nodded and lumbered away. David didn't

know what he did for lunch. It didn't really matter. Even after a week of working for him, he'd hardly gotten any more words out of the man. It didn't bother him, though. The quiet was good. A place with no expectations, really.

Well, that wasn't true. He was expected to work, and he worked. And he got paid.

And for lunch he went to Candide.

He slipped onto what had become his stool. Major dropped a plate of beans and stew onto the bar and poured him a beer. David placed a dime on the counter.

And Maggie sat next to him. "You stink, Davey."

"Working will do that." His ears burned, but not nearly so much as they used to.

"You smell better than most men, even with all that sweat."

"Yeah. Well." He scraped some beans into his mouth. He felt so dirty sitting next to her. He missed her. He missed the way they used to talk. She deserved so much better. Any of the men she took care of would be better than him. What was he thinking, coming in here every day?

"Stop that." She leaned on the bar. "You're thinking again."

He looked over at her.

"I can tell. You always get that little crinkle between your eyes when you're thinking." She reached over and gently touched the space between his eyebrows. "Right there."

She touched him. His fingers twitched. He dropped the spoon. Bean juice splattered. Maggie laughed.

He laughed, too.

"You know you're the only man who doesn't have to buy time from me," she said.

His fingers twitched again.

"I mean, I like spending time with you. Remembering. And I like your laugh." She leaned close and whispered, "And I don't mind how sweaty you are."

Her breath caressed his ear. Once more he was burning.

"I can't, Maggie. I can't." He pushed the half-eaten plate away. "You don't know. I shouldn't be here at all. I should leave."

She grabbed his arm. "Davey, why are you running away?"

He looked away. "I'm a soldier now, Mags."

"Yeah?"

"I did things that were bad. Wrong."

"Yeah? Have you seen what I do? Look at my dress. Come on. Look at me."

He forced his head to turn to look at her. At all of her, dress and all. Once his eyes landed on her chest, he couldn't look anywhere else. He felt his face turn redder and redder. She hadn't let him see or touch her like that before he left for the war. Now...

He looked back up.

"If I can show you this much of me and not be scared, if you don't mind sitting here day after day next to me, if you're not ashamed of me, I won't be ashamed of you, Davey."

He squeezed his eyes shut. He couldn't tell her. Not really. It was so hard to breathe.

"Davey. I'm not ashamed of you."

He exhaled. "We were supposed to clear out a forest. Someplace out east. I don't even know where. Somewhere out there. Rebels were in there. We went in. And... and the forest didn't like us. I was the only one who got out, Mags. Everyone else." He felt the tears coming. His shoulders twitched. "I should go. Ezra'll be expecting me back."

Maggie nodded slowly. "Come back to me?"

"Why?"

"Because you don't think I'm dirty, and you're not here just because you want something from me."

He gave a stiff nod and headed back to the smithy.

8.

The metal jangled in the wagon. Jarvis had wanted a stove, all fancy. Something about wanting something for his new wife.

Another new wife. Jarvis went through them faster than... well, faster than something. Ezra wasn't good with comparisons. A thing was a thing. You didn't need to say it was like something else.

The horses pulled the heavy wagon. Ezra sat at the front, driving them. David took care of the smith today. Should be fine. He was a fine man. Kept a good rhythm at the bellows, and he was learning how to handle a hammer. He was clumsy. Never be good at it, but he'd be good enough to pound out simple things. Jumpy, though.

The horses clomped along, their hooves pressing into the dirt. They provided a good beat. Ezra leaned into that beat, letting his heart match the pulse. He scanned the distant horizon.

Well, he tried to. The trees got in the way.

Trees?

There hadn't been trees here last time he rode out to Jarvis's. The ranch had some trees by the houses, and a few stunted ones out where the cattle grazed, but nothing like this. Ezra couldn't see the mountains. Thick green leaves hid the sun. It suddenly felt cool in the shade. The trunks of the trees grew crooked and thick.

The blacksmith glanced around. Trees don't suddenly appear, do they? Not normally. A tree stood still. It just grew out of the ground and stayed in one place. At least a good tree did that. These must not be good trees, then.

But Jarvis needed the stove. Well, maybe not, but he was paying for it, and that was good enough. The horses didn't act nervous. They just kept pressing on.

Well, he trusted horses. Animals with good sense, usually, as long as they weren't panicked. And these animals weren't panicked.

He eased back into the rhythm of the hooves. Jarvis's shouldn't be that far. Hard to tell with all the trees in the way, but he'd be there before noon. Plenty of time to install the stove.

Ezra didn't notice the bleached skull staring at him from among the branches.

It took him all day to install the stove. He bunked with the hands that night and hitched the horses the next morning. No metal jangling in the wagon this time.

And no trees on the way home.

9.

He had to tell someone. The pressure had been building. He was so alone in his fear. But every time he thought about opening his mouth, every time he thought that maybe he should tell Ezra or Major, he thought about what they'd do. He thought about how he'd lose his job. He wouldn't be welcome in Can-dide. And telling Mama? Of course not. He couldn't do that to her.

But Maggie said she wasn't ashamed of him.

It took a long time for the thought to finally really come to him. It shouldn't have surprised him. It was Mags. It was his girl. It didn't matter how many men knew her. Mags and Davey...

He'd seen how it worked often enough. At lunch, when she sat on the stool next to him, he looked at her. "How much?" he stuttered.

Her face lit up. "Three dollars."

"I got enough."

She took his hand and guided him off the stool. She led him to the stairs.

He tripped on the bottom one and almost landed on his face.

The girls on the balcony burst into laughter. "'Bout time you got him!" yelled one. Several of the men at the tables joined in the mockery. David's ears blazed.

"Don't pay them no mind," Maggie said. "They're just jeal-ous."

She finally got him up the stairs and took him down a narrow hall. She opened the third door on the left and motioned him in.

The narrow room held a bed with a few blankets and pillows on it. The walls were plain wood. No window; just an unlit lamp. Once David stepped in, Maggie lit a match, and the lamp gave off warm light. She shut the door.

"I've wanted this for so long. Since before you left." She reached to unbutton his shirt.

He looked down at her. At her dress. Thought about how of-ten he'd wanted it, too. How much he'd wanted to see her with-out her clothes, to know what it would be like to be not just with any woman, but with her.

But she should know. She should know how dirty he was. His fingers twitched. He didn't want to pollute her. She meant far, far too much to him. He took a careful step back and bumped into the wall. "I can't."

"I'll be gentle." She reached for his shirt again.

He burst into tears. A sob shook his body. He crumpled for-ward, his forehead resting on her bare shoulder. "No. No! You deserve better. So much better. I just… I need to tell you."

"You did." Her arms wrapped around him. "You're not the first man to cry when he comes up here. It's the only safe place for a lot of men."

"No. I didn't tell you. Just let me. Please? Just let me."

She stepped away. "All right, Davey. If that's what you need."

He opened his mouth. This was his chance, to finally let it out. To finally release everything that had happened to him.

But what would happen if she rejected him? She said she wasn't ashamed of him.

But she didn't know. How could she? How could anyone know?

Another sob shook him. "It was the forest. The rebels were hiding in there."

"You told me."

"They were just kids, Mags. Just kids." And the words finally poured out. He couldn't stop them. "They should've been going to school, playing tricks on their teachers or something. They should've been hunting with their dads, not fighting with guns. And I shot them. I killed them, Mags. Not all of them. But I did. I shot." He sobbed again.

She reached for him, but he shook his head so hard he might have strained something in his neck. "The forest didn't like it. The branches groaned. They shook at us. And the trees attacked all the men with me. All of them. I can't." He squeezed his eyes shut. More tears poured out as he once more heard the sound of flesh bursting and branches growing. "And the forest's been chasing me ever since. That's why I can't stay."

"Davey, you've been here for over a month."

"How fast does a forest travel?"

"Trees don't move, Davey."

"These ones did."

She didn't answer for a long time. They stood there in the dark room. He sobbed again, and again.

Finally, she took him by the hand and laid him on the bed. She lay next to him, her head on his shoulder. He wrapped his arms around her. Once his tears stopped, they finally slept.

10.

When they woke, Maggie undressed him. She slipped her dress off. They made love.

It wasn't as good as David had always dreamed. He thought it would be magical. It wasn't, really.

But it was her. After, as they held each other, that's what was good. He gently kissed her forehead. "I love you," he whispered.

"I know." She nuzzled into his neck. "I love you."

They fell asleep again.

He jerked awake. "What time is it?" He'd never been late before. Of course he'd be late for Ezra. Would the blacksmith fire him?

Maggie stirred. "That's the best I've ever slept with a man." She gazed up at him. "I'm safe with you."

"What time is it?" He flailed out of bed. "I need to get back to work." He tangled in the sheets and lost his balance, falling back onto the mattress.

Maggie wrapped her arms around him. "I don't know what time it is. But I love you."

He wanted to weep. He wanted to sing. He didn't have time for this. He should make time for it. He couldn't figure out what to say.

They'd finally done it. And she loved him. He should take her away. He could take care of her, right?

No. She needed someone better.

Words. Words were so hard, and emotions were more difficult. He wished he was marching or pumping the bellows or something that didn't involve him having to deal with this woman that he loved, that he needed to get away from, that he couldn't leave ever, ever again.

"I don't know what time it is. There ain't no clocks in Candide. Major's rule." She stretched.

David stared. He couldn't look away. Just look at her. Look at how good she looked. He needed to hurry, but as much as she'd looked good in the dress, she looked even better out of her dress, just sitting in that bed.

She smiled at him. "Do you have to go?"

He tried to find words. Well, he wanted to stop thinking.

Staring at her was a good way to do that, he guessed.

She scooted toward him. "You can stay with me as long as you want." She gave a mischievous smile.

His fingers twitched. "I'm coming back. Don't let any other man in here, okay?" He felt dirty just asking it. He didn't have any claim on her. How could he?

But she didn't turn him away. She'd accepted him, even after he told her what he'd done. She held him close. She allowed him to be here. She said she loved him.

"Even after what I did?"

She scooted toward him. "Davey, I don't know what it takes to be a soldier. But I know that people do what they got to. And I ain't ashamed of you. Look at you. Coming in every day to have lunch with a whore, but you weren't scared to eat with me. You weren't ashamed of me. How could I be ashamed of you?"

He was going to burst into tears again. He was going to throw himself on top of her and make love again. He had to go. He had to stay.

She finally made up his mind for him by taking him by the hand and laying him back on the bed.

11.

Now it was way, way too late. David jerked awake, rolled out of bed, and yanked on his pants. Ezra was definitely going to get rid of him. Was it already so late that his mama would be angry?

"Come back to me?" Maggie asked.

He leaned over the bed and kissed her fiercely. "Yes." The second the word left his mouth, he felt guilty. He shouldn't come back to her.

He loved her.

She loved him.

He had to get home.

He threw his shirt on and buttoned it up as fast as his fingers could travel, even as they twitched. He grinned at her. She was still amazing. "I wish we were married so I could come back to you every night."

She sat up. "Do you mean that?"

Did he?

"Yeah. Yeah, I do."

She leaped from the bed and threw her arms around him. "Come back to me," she whispered into his ear. "We'll get married, like we should have before you left." She kissed him fiercely.

He almost took her back to the bed. Instead, he stepped out of the room and rushed down the stairs. The bar was abandoned. No piano player. No Major behind the bar. No girls on the balcony.

The dim light of dawn shone through the windows.

David groaned. Mama was going to kill him. She wouldn't care about his upcoming marriage. Actually, she'd probably yell at him for marrying a whore.

Well, who cared what she thought? He was going to get married. He was going to finally marry the girl he was always supposed to marry. Sure, he was filthy with his past. Sure, she deserved so much better than him.

But she loved him.

She loved him!

He still couldn't get that thought to stick. It was a wonder. He stumbled across the bar to get to the doors and stepped outside.

The air was chilly. The sky shone pale blue, with bright red in the east. He grinned. A beautiful start to a beautiful day. He'd have to find that parson. What did Mama say his name was?

But first he should go home. He should let Mama know he was fine. Hopefully she didn't wake up Sheriff Carter last night in a panic.

Mama really would be angry at him. A good boy doesn't spend the night with a whore. She'd be hurt and furious and relieved when she saw him.

But right now, he was so happy, he told himself he didn't care. He'd hug Mama and tell her it was going to be all right and he was getting married and she couldn't say no and he'd go and take Maggie and everything would be good.

She loved him.

He crossed Main Street and made his way to Mama's house along the top of the T. He passed the abandoned train station and began whistling. A few people moved already. Some men rode by on horses. They touched their hats as they passed.

David nodded back.

And then there was Mama's house.

It was fine. She'd be angry, but it would be fine. His fingers twitched.

No. None of that. This was a happy day. A good day. He stepped forward and swung open the door. "Mama!"

No one answered.

She must have fallen asleep. He peaked into her room.

The bed was empty.

He frowned. Maybe she'd gone out looking for him? At dawn she'd usually be up making breakfast, but she wasn't in the kitchen either. He poked his head out the back door.

He vomited.

He'd seen dead bodies before, of course. He'd seen friends ripped apart by bullets and shattered by canon shot.

But he'd never imagined seeing his mama hanging from a tree branch.

12.

By the time he'd run and brought Doc Jasper, the tree was gone. Of course it was.

Mama's eyes bulged. Dark marks wrapped around her neck. She lay on the dusty ground.

Doc Jasper leaned over her. "Yep. She's been dead a while, David. Odd, though. Go get the sheriff, would you?"

He nodded and obeyed. A good soldier obeys.

The sheriff scratched his head. "Looks like someone hung her."

"That's what I thought," Doc Jasper answered. He peered around. "Nothing here to hang her from, though."

"I hate weird shit." Carter spat. "Far as I know, no one was mad at Hattie. You know of anyone angry enough to hang her?"

David shook his head. No one was angry at Mama. Well, maybe Maggie, but that's because Mama could be mean sometimes. Say things. Judge people. But Maggie wouldn't kill anyone.

No. The trees did this. They weren't angry at Mama, though. They were angry at him.

The sheriff knelt. "Well, call up Clive. He's got someone else to take care of. Hopefully the parson can bury her right."

David leaned back against the house. His hands twitched. His shoulders shook.

Mama.

He shouldn't have been happy. The forest knew. It was still coming for him. What was he thinking, staying here so long? It found him. It found Mama.

It was going to find Maggie.

He dashed away. The sheriff called after him. He didn't listen, though. He had to make sure Maggie was okay. He sprinted down Main Street. It was way busier now. Of course it was. He dodged around a wagon and into a horse's path. He lurched to avoid it. The rider cursed. He just kept moving.

He burst through Candide's door. The piano faltered. The girls gasped. He raced past the bar. Major called out a greeting. He didn't answer it. He sprinted up the steps.

She had to be okay. She had to be fine. The forest couldn't find Maggie.

Third door on the left. He threw it open.

She sat on the bed in a fine Sunday dress. She grinned up at him. "Davey!"

He swept her up into his arms. All of him shook. He sobbed. "You're okay. You're okay!"

"Of course I am! Just been waiting for you. We gotta go get the parson!" And then she realized that David wasn't fine. "What's wrong? Davey, what's wrong?"

"The forest got Mama," he finally wheezed out.

"What?"

"The forest. It hung her. It caught up. It's going to get me. I just had to see. You're fine. You're okay."

"I've just been here. Of course I'm fine. It'll take more than some trees to get me." She squeezed him.

"I need to leave. I need to go before it gets you." He pulled away.

"No! No, Davey. You hear me? You're not going anywhere without me. We finally found each other. I'm not losing you again." She seized his hand and would not let go.

"And I'm not losing you. Not again. I'm leaving so you can

keep going."

"Davey. Davey, look at me. You're going to be my husband. And wherever you go, I'm going, too. If the forest is going to get you, it's going to get both of us. And if you want to keep me safe, then you'll have to keep safe, too."

He couldn't answer.

"Come on. Let's get the parson. I don't have much here to pack. You're used to traveling light, soldier. We'll be fine on the road. You and me, the way it was always supposed to be."

13.

It took less than two minutes for Maggie to gather up what she wanted to bring. "I ain't taking that dress," she said, kicking her revealing outfit. "Ain't got to show off for no one but you no more."

David grinned. He stammered, but finally got out, "I like you in nothing at all." His ears burned.

She kissed him. "We're getting married, and then you can see me naked all you want."

"We ain't ever gonna get anything done then."

She winked.

They made their way down the steps. The girls looked on, confused. Maggie stopped at the bar. "Thanks for watching out for me, Major."

He grinned. "You two heading off into the sunset?"

"That's the plan," she answered.

"Well, come here and give me a hug!"

"No way, old man." She raised a finger. "I belong with Davey now!"

He nodded. "All right then. Safe rides!" He lifted a mug of beer to toast them.

David stepped to the door and peered at the street. "Looks safe," he said.

"Then let's go. We got to get that parson."

He nodded. "Let's get to the chapel." He felt a pang.

The parson would be burying Mama this afternoon, wouldn't he? And David would be riding off with the love of his life, not even here for the funeral. Maybe he should stay.

No. No, he couldn't. The trees would find him. They'd find Maggie. He had to ride away. Nothing else to be done. He shouldn't even be stopping to get married. They could get a parson at the next town over. Or they could just say they were married.

He looked over at Maggie. She walked beside him.

No. She deserved something real, and something now. They could risk this. Maybe. Hopefully. After all, if the trees had already found Mama, waiting these extra few minutes to get married wouldn't cause any more hardship. Hopefully. His fingers twitched.

"The town looks different in the morning," Maggie said.

"What?"

"Oh, I'm usually in the bar except at dark. Don't get to see people like this."

"You're okay with them judging you?"

She winked. "Most people don't look at my face in the bar. They probably don't know who I am. And if someone knows who I am, just ask them how they know."

"Mama knew what you were doing."

"Well, someone told her then, didn't they?" She laughed, but even in the laugh David could hear some of that defensiveness.

"I don't care." He took her hand. "You're going to be my wife. I love you. I never judged you. And you never judged me. I guess we were made for each other."

"I guess we were." She grinned.

His heart leaped. It fell. Mama dead. He was getting married. He was running away. He was running away with the woman he loved. Too many emotions all over the place.

But he knew that marrying Maggie was right.

They walked out of town, her hand through his arm. The chapel was right ahead of them. The sun shone above.

And then something hid the sun. He looked up. Leaves shaded them. Trees all around.

The forest had found him.

14.

His friends were already dead. There was no way he could be

hearing the sounds of roots burrowing under skin or branches growing through eye sockets. He couldn't hear his friends screaming out in pain and horror. It wasn't real. They were already gone.

But the forest was here.

The light dimmed, darker, darker. The leaves thickened above until only a green darkness filtered around them. Though there was no breeze, the leaves clapped together in joy. They'd finally found him. The last one that had displeased them so much.

David squeezed his eyes shut. "Mags, go home. Go home now. Maybe the trees will let you through. All they want is me."

"No!" She spun around, trying to look at the entire forest in one glance. "No. You're the only person that's not ashamed of me. I'm not leaving you."

"You have to! I thought we had time. I was wrong." He blinked through his tears. "It wants me, and it's right. I killed children, Mags. I'm not someone you should ever be with. I deserve to be ripped apart. I deserve this." His fingers spasmed. His shoulders twitched. When had he fallen to his knees? He didn't remember falling. He stood and turned, looking at all the trees.

The trunks grew thicker, the branches more gnarled. The temperature plummeted.

"They can have me," David said.

"No! They can't. You don't belong to the trees. I don't care what you did. You belong with me!" Maggie sobbed. "I won't let the forest take you."

The leaves grew in volume. Branches clacked against each other. The ground rumbled as roots dug through it.

"He belongs with me!" she shouted.

David tried to stand between her and the trees, but there was no way to do it. He circled her. "Let her go! Take me! I'm the one you want!" He had to shout to be heard over the sound of the trees.

The branches spread their fingers toward them, reaching down from above, from the left, from the right, all around them.

"You can't have him!" Maggie shouted.

The leaves fell silent. The branches held still. The only sound was their breathing.

A hoof struck the ground. Another hoof. Out of the green darkness a form emerged. It had four legs like a deer. Its tiny tail flicked. Its mold-colored hide stuck to its ribs. A human torso rose from it, its skin the color of willow bark, its fingers long enough to almost touch the ground. A buck's skull sat atop its shoulders. Its antlers spread wider than a person could stretch their arms. It turned its empty eye sockets on David.

His fingers twitched. "I'm... Uh, I'm the one you want."

"No. I am!" Maggie flung herself between them.

The creature raised a finger and pointed at David. "It belongs to me."

15.

Parson Dies never figured out where the trees had come from. Two of them stood beside the road to the chapel now. If he squinted, they almost looked like two people had sprouted branches and leaves.

He shrugged. There were enough weird things in town. He had worse things to think about than where two trees had come from.

THE LANDOWNER

1.

The sun seemed to blaze hotter than it ever had the day the Landowner came to town. He walked from the west. The gravel crunched under his dark boots. His dark suit and dark hat didn't seem to bother him, though it must have felt like a furnace under those layers of clothing. He wore no weapon anyone could see, but he walked with a confidence that said nothing bothered him. Nothing at all.

He walked Main Street, eyeing the buildings and examining the people. The women shivered as his gaze swept by them. The men hunched their shoulders and walked more quickly to whatever errand they pursued.

The man smiled as he stood in the middle of the road. "It's been a year. Time's up." He considered where to begin. Finally, he turned to the blacksmith.

2.

Ezra had gone back to pumping his own bellows. He missed that David. He'd pumped well. Set up a good rhythm. Didn't talk too much. That's exactly what he wanted. He stopped pumping when the stranger stepped into the shop, though. He stood and waited for the man in the dark suit to speak.

The man eyed the building, and then he looked Ezra up and down. "This is my land. It's time you paid rent."

Ezra raised a bushy eyebrow.

"I know. You've forgotten. It was part of the deal. But the year is over. Payment is due. The land is mine. It wasn't here until the white man arrived. Didn't you find it curious that no natives ever visit here? Where do you think the land came from? I provided it. For you. And now, well, it's time to pay up. I am the Landowner. What will you pay?"

The blacksmith shook his head. Some sort of joke he didn't understand, clearly.

"I know why you stay quiet, Ezra. I know that talking's your most dangerous enemy. Once you start, you just don't stop, do you?"

Ezra felt a tension in his shoulders.

"And you have this way of seeing things. Everyone else thinks that everything is like something else, but you. You see the truth of the matter. So when you talk, you speak the truth, and that makes people uncomfortable. And uncomfortable people make life so difficult, don't they? Especially when they know what you really think of them."

"Don't know what you're talking about," he said, his voice gruff. He found a hammer in his hand.

"Of course not. And yet, you owe me. What will you pay?"

"Out." He pointed.

"Or what?" The man in black grinned. "Will you tell me what you really think? Oh, put the hammer down. You can't do anything to me unless I let you. And you won't like what I do to you."

Ezra made himself as big as he could. He stepped closer, looming over the smaller man. His grip strengthened on the hammer.

"Oh, my. Well, I suppose you'll just need to talk now."

Ezra sneered. And then his mouth popped open. "I'm scared all the time." He froze. "Everyone knows what they're doing, but I don't. So if I keep quiet, maybe they'll think I'm smart. Maybe they'll never know how little I really am."

He dropped the hammer and slapped a hand over his mouth. The words tumbled past his fingers.

"Not like Daddy. Daddy always made fun of me. So did Kevin. The first time he saw me naked, he pointed and laughed and laughed and he said I'd never screw a girl because I wasn't big enough."

Something inside him quivered. A sob slipped out between the words.

"I wanted to kill him, but he ran away and told Dad and he beat me and he beat me so hard and I'm not good enough. I wish I was. I wish I was big and strong and maybe everyone will think that I am if I just hammer and hammer and do everything I'm supposed to do."

He tried roaring. He tried swearing. He tried saying anything but what he did. He tried saying anything that wasn't true. Something that wasn't what he was actually scared of. Something so he could pretend this was just a joke.

"And as long as I don't screw any women, I'll never have to worry about whether or not I'm really big enough or if they'll laugh like Kevin did. But Kevin was so much bigger than me and he took me out behind the barn one day and he proved it and I kind of liked it, but I can't tell anyone that. I wish I was big like him and strong and knew just what to do all the time. I wanted to tear his dick off and nail it to my crotch so I could finally be a man like him."

Ezra gagged. He spat. The words, though. They just kept coming and coming and coming.

"I finally did it, you know. Kevin got drunk. And I was starting to learn my trade. I heated up some shears real hot. And I snuck up on him. He screamed so loud. But I was finally bigger than him."

The Landowner nodded. "Well. See that you're at the train station at midnight. I have more debts to collect." He exited the shop.

Ezra, though, fell to his knees, sobbing, sobbing, saying all the terrible things he'd done so long ago. The last words that the Landowner heard as he left were, "And I don't even care. Kevin deserved it. I'm proud of what I did. Everyone would think it's terrible, but it's beautiful what I did to him."

3.

He entered Candide next. So many debts to collect here. He looked around the room. Just a few men lingering over their lunches. The girls on the balcony perked up when he walked through the doors. The bartender with the huge handlebar mustache set a glass on the counter. "Hey, stranger. What can I get for you?"

The man in black seated himself on a stool. "None of that. Your girls. That's what I'm here for."

Major Ellis beamed. "Well, every man's got a need, don't he? Take your pick. Each one'll treat you fine."

"You misunderstand me, Major. You owe me. If you give me your girls, all of them, I'll allow you to stay in Scar Ridge." He waved a hand. "I wouldn't worry if I were you. There are always more girls, aren't there?"

"Allow me to stay in Scar Ridge?" Ellis's face darkened. "Sir, perhaps you should leave."

The Landowner chuckled. "No, no, this is my land, and I decide who stays or goes. You have racked up quite a debt. I am being quite generous, though. I could demand that you pay personally. I suspect you wouldn't enjoy that. Instead, you simply, willingly, give up the girls. Each one of them. I'll take them away under my care."

"They're my girls. I'll take care of them. You won't do anything to them."

"Come, you don't need to pretend to be virtuous. I know the truth. I know how you treat each of those girls like they're special. You treat them like they're your own wives, every one of them. After all, you should sample the goods before you sell to your patrons." He shrugged. "That's nothing new for a man in your business. It is a shame that some of those girls are actually your daughters, though."

The color drained from the bartender's face.

"What lies did you tell those girls? Do they even know that you're their father? You did get around a fair bit in your youth, didn't you?"

Ellis trembled. "How do you know?" he whispered.

"My land. I know everything that goes on. I know everyone who lives here. And as I said, I'm here to collect debts. I am a man of my word. If you choose not to pay with your girls, I will tell everyone in town what you've done. Of course, if I take the girls away, I won't say a word. Your little business here will continue to sell joy in all its many colors."

4.

The Landowner stepped into the room after the girl. It was a small space, filled mostly with a bed. "Well. I see what you must spend most of your time doing."

The girl shrugged. "It's what I'm good at." She stepped close to him. "Want me to show you?"

"Do you like it?"

She blinked for just a moment before reaching up to caress his cheek. "Why wouldn't I?"

"I own the land that Candide is built on. Major needs to pay. And he has decided to pay with you."

A sharp intake of breath before she said, "Well, I can take care of you." She ran her fingers through his hair.

"Well, you can if you wish, but my tastes run a very different way." He stepped away. "No. I've come to take you away, if you'd like it. He'll pay with you. Not with an hour or a night. You come with me. The truth is I could force you to come with, but for you, for you I'm willing to give you a choice."

She blinked up at him. "I could leave?"

"Of course. This is your choice. You can stay here, living out your days until no man will pay to be with you. You know what will happen then."

She backed away, her arms wrapped around her stomach. "It happened to Millie. She couldn't pay her rent to Major no more. He kicked her out." Tears threatened to tumble down her cheeks. "I tried paying for her, but she wouldn't let me. She walked out the door one day. No one's seen her since."

"Ah, Millie. Yes." He lifted his chin. "I remember her. She made a deal with me, too. I took her away so she wouldn't ever have to work for Major again."

The girl shivered. "I don't wanna work for him. He's not as kind as he likes people to think he is."

"Oh, I am quite aware. And if I take you away, you'll never have to work for him again. You'll work for me."

"What will I do for you?"

The Landowner flashed a smile. "Not anything involving sex.

Unless, of course, you preferred that. I'm sure we could find some sort of work for you that involved that part of your body. The simple truth is most of my compatriots are not interested in sex. No. We do have need of people who can work with their hands, though. Do you know how to knit?"

She searched the floor, remembering. "I used to. Mama had me work with her."

"So you could be taught."

"Oh, yes! I can learn real good."

He nodded. "Then it's settled. You'll knit for me if you come with me. Or you can choose to stay until you get too old and no man wants you anymore. And let's face it, you're not that far away."

"I'm only nineteen!"

"Oh, are you? Have you looked in a mirror recently? You appear far older."

The girl glanced around. "Where would I look in a mirror?"

The Landowner reached into a pocket and pulled out a glass. "Look here."

She took it from him, eager to see what she looked like. She raised a trembling hand to her face. "Wrinkles? When did I get wrinkles?"

"It's a hard life, doing what you do."

"They're getting worse!"

"Of course they are."

"My hair's falling out!"

The man in black examined his fingernails. "So it is. I am sorry, but I am busy today. I have been kind enough to give you a choice, but I must move on. Will you stay here, or will you knit for me?"

Her hands trembled. "I'll come with you." Her voice scratched.

"Very good." He nodded. "Be at the train station at midnight. I'm glad you'll be joining us. Not many of my people can handle the screams."

"Screams?"

He plucked the mirror from her hands. "Oh yes. The screams. We don't use wool for knitting where I'm from. And very few people have hair we could use. So we use intestines."

She wrinkled her nose.

"From people, my dear. From living people. A bloody business, knitting, but you've agreed to it. Now I must move on. Midnight at the train station! Don't be late. You won't be happy if you're left behind, believe me!"

5.

Another girl, another room. All of them so far had chosen to go with the Landowner. No surprise. They couldn't imagine anything worse than Major running their lives. Hope was such a powerful drug.

This girl had long blonde hair done up in ringlets and little braids, all fancy. Her pale blue dress showed off her ample chest. She pressed up against him and ran a finger over one of his ears. "What would you like?" she whispered.

"Not what you're offering," he answered. "I've been around so long, I'm sure you wouldn't be interested in anything I might want."

"Try me." She giggled. "I hear you've been offering the other girls all sorts of things. I want to show you how valuable I could be to you." She leaned in and breathed into his ear, "I could do things for you. I could be anyone you wanted." She leaned back and winked. "One guy who visits me likes me to pretend to be his mommy. Another likes my name to be Hilda." She shrugged. "So whatever you want me to be, I'll be."

"Well." He chuckled. "If that's what you want to offer me…"

She licked her lips. "Anything. Anyone."

He nodded. "Well, we'll have to make some adjustments if that's what you want to be." He stepped back and looked her up and down. "First, your chest is far too large for my liking."

She gasped, grabbing her dress as it almost fell off her. She stared down at herself. "I ain't been this flat since I was ten!"

"And your skin. Far too white."

She began scratching at her arms, her throat, her face. Black bristles sprouted over her skin, even as that skin darkened. She screeched. Her dress slipped off her entirely, but she didn't even notice as she stared at her skin. All of her was turning blacker than the night sky, and being covered with those wiry hairs.

"Now, we must do something about that rear of yours."

Her butt expanded. She lost her balance and landed on it. She yelped in pain, but it grew and grew. Soon it was as large as her torso, sticking out behind her, a huge sack of fat. It came to a point.

"Closer. Your legs are too long."

She fell forward now as her thighs cracked and snapped and tore apart. The flesh reknit around them. Her toes separated. She wept as her arms separated. She pushed herself up off the floor as much as she could. She squinted, or tried to. Her eyelids were gone.

"You wanted to please me. This is at least closer to what I like." He gestured. "Somewhat like a spider, I suppose. Let me look at you."

She tried to cover her body, but her flesh would not bend the way she was used to. Anything she valued had been stripped away and twisted and perverted and all she wanted to do was hide.

"No. Not pretty enough for me," he sighed. "Nor for anyone ever again, I suspect. Would you prefer to stay here, or would you like to run away with me?"

She trembled. She sobbed. In the end she chose to go with him. There would be nothing for her here now.

6.

His business at Candide complete, the Landowner moved on to Danzig's. He admired the walls as he entered. "A new construction? I'm impressed. Who'd you piss off this time?"

Hilda hissed from behind the counter. "I've paid my price!" she screamed.

"You have. I can't touch you for many years to come. Your grandson, though. He has not paid the price. Where is Bart?"

As he asked, the old man wandered in from the back room. He grinned as he saw the man in black. "Hey, mister. You new in town? Whatever you want, we got it here."

Hilda put a hand on his chest. "You need to go home now."

"No. No he doesn't." The Landowner gave a lazy grin. "He'd

rather come play with me."

"No! You can't take him!"

"Why not?"

Bart blinked. A grin spread on his face. "Yeah! I'd rather come play. The old lady always makes me work here. I never get to go run around with the other kids! Course, they think I'm an old guy. We really fooled them!" He frowned for a moment. "I forgot. I forgot I was a kid." He shook his head. "But I am a kid! I fooled everyone!"

"You sure did, Bart." The man in black nodded. "I was almost fooled. But your grandma's been playing this game for a long time. She gave you her age, she took your youth. Nice trade. You get everything you ever wanted, and she gets everything she always wanted."

Hilda swore at him.

Bart's eyes got real big. "You never say that kind of stuff!"

"Do you want to be a kid again, Bart?" the Landowner asked. "For real?"

"Yeah. It's fun being an adult and doing grown-up stuff, but I'd like to play again."

"Come with me." He held out a hand.

"Bart, no!"

The old man took a step around the counter. "I get to play again!" His white hair turned dark. Another step, and his beard grew back into his face. "I can't wait to play tag!" His voice cracked. Another step, and his clothes were too large for him. "It'll be so good!" Another, and he was too young for school. He giggled. He landed on his face in front of the Landowner and began bawling.

The man in black reached down and plucked up the toddler. No, infant, now.

Hilda trembled. "He belongs to me."

"Oh, he won't belong to anyone, soon." The newborn screamed. "Of course, you could give him some of your age. You'd be younger yet, but that shouldn't bother you. What's a few more years?"

Hilda spat. "It's not fair."

"You sound like the young woman you pretend to be. You know the world is not fair. It belongs to people like me. And now it's too late for your grandson."

Bart was gone.

"You'll need to find another child to give your age to. Until next time." He tipped his hat and stepped out into the street.

7.

It didn't take too long for the Landowner to walk to Jarvis's ranch. The old man waited for him on the steps.

"Time to pay up," the man in black said.

Jarvis nodded. He called to the hands. They all gathered around the cattle in the yard. Many of them wept, but they had all been told. There was a price to living in Scar Ridge.

The man in black waited patiently.

Eventually the hands began driving the cattle to town.

"Yes. These are so much tastier to me and my friends. The meat has such feeling in it. Much better than any other cattle. So much tastier if they've been loved, the way you love them. Keep loving them deeply, every wife that comes here, so it hurts when I come back for them every year."

Jarvis growled, "I know the deal."

"I don't think you've obeyed it, though." He turned his face toward the second floor of the big house. "There's someone else in there."

"I don't know what you're talking about."

"Never lie to a liar, Jarvis. I've allowed you extra time with her, but that first wife of yours belongs to me. Unless, of course, you'd rather pay a different price?"

"You broke your end of the deal. We hardly got to know these women. Didn't have more than a month or two with them before they began to change."

"Watch your tone, or next time they'll begin changing on your wedding night. Imagine if your hands were having fun with a woman and then suddenly the women had udders!" The Landowner laughed. "Oh, I might do that just for fun."

Jarvis threw a punch. It connected with the Landowner's jaw. He flinched under the assault. Jarvis came in to strike his stomach and then around to the jaw again. One of the hands saw and called out. The rest of the hands moved in to join the fray, beating the Landowner down. They called to each other, egged each other on. The man in black fell on his knees. Blood ran down his chin. Someone kicked him in the stomach. He collapsed to the ground. He lay still.

The hands looked around at each other, panting.

Jarvis stared down at the man. "That's it? That's all it took?" He stepped back. "We could've done that years ago." He shook.

The hands looked up at him. "We coulda?" one asked.

"Look! Just a man." His voice was filled with wonder. "I don't know how, but all it took was us beating him. He didn't even fight back." He thought of Mathilde. He thought of Maria and Katie and the other wives that he'd loved despite himself, all of them sacrificed to this Landowner, all those wasted lives.

And that's what the hands thought of, too. They narrowed their eyes. "You knew?"

"Hell, no." Jarvis shook his head.

"But you never tried before. You could've, but you didn't." Another hand stepped close. "I lost two wives. But I didn't have to? If you'd just stood up to him before?"

"You saw him. You've seen what he could do!" Jarvis stepped back.

"You didn't even try."

He stuttered. He hadn't tried.

The hands muttered. They crowded around.

Jarvis pulled his pistol first. The hands followed suit. A flurry of shots followed. Screaming as the survivors bled out.

The man in black stood and brushed the dust off his suit. "Well, that was invigorating. I'll have to find another rancher to raise my cattle, though." He looked over at the cows. "Come on. You have a train waiting for you."

8.

Sheriff Carter stepped into the street. His hand rested lightly on his pistol's grip. He narrowed his eyes.

The Landowner strolled back into town whistling a jaunty tune.

"I beat you last time," Carter growled.

"Certainly, you did." The man in black stuck his hands in his pockets. "And you've had your year. I don't think I'll be playing any games this time. I learned, you see."

"You can't take the town. Not again." He kept the tremor from his voice.

"Oh, Sheriff, you think any of this is my fault?" He put a hand to his chest, his eyes wide. "I am innocent of anything you could accuse me of. I am simply calling in debts that have been created. I am owed." He cocked his head. "And what do you owe, Sheriff?"

"Not a thing."

He sighed. "I suppose that's true. You don't, do you? Everyone else in this town makes deals. You, though, you do your best to do the right thing. I don't like it. I have no claim on you." He shook his head. "Unless, of course, you get in my way. And you wouldn't want to do that."

"No, I do not." His hand remained on the pistol. "But a man's got to do what a man's got to do."

"Are you planning on shooting me?"

"If I have to." Carter hoped he sounded more confident than he felt. "I've shot you before."

"You have. And you've seen that it does nothing."

"I gotta do something."

The Landowner pulled back the edge of his suit jacket, revealing a holster at his hip. "Trust me when I say that I move faster than you've ever thought of moving. You pull that little gun on me, you'll be dead before your corpse touches the ground."

"Big words."

"Real words. I get called a lot of things, of course, but I'm not much for lying. Despite what some people might say about me. I find that the truth is so much more dangerous than a lie."

The two men regarded each other. A breeze wafted through the street. No one else moved. The sun sank lower.

Carter's hand darted up. The pistol flashed.

He dropped to the ground.

"A shame." The Landowner slipped his pistol back into its holster. "He really fought for his people. It would have been far better to keep him here. A challenge. Oh, well."

He continued whistling his tune, stepping around the body

as he went on his way.

9.

The Landowner strolled out to the chapel. Last stop for the evening. The sun had just set, its last rays lingering in the west. He passed two trees on the way. He paused, looked them up and down, and shook his head. "Claimed by another. Too bad." He continued on his way.

He passed the chapel without a second thought. At the edge of All Saints graveyard, he clapped his hands.

The dead rose.

"No rest until your debts are paid. You can't escape me that way. To the train station!"

The dead lamented their lives. A woman in a floral print dress stumbled by, tears streaming down her face. "He was a good man, wasn't he? Didn't he lay me down? I just want to sleep. Just sleep."

First four people passed the Landowner on their way to town, then a dozen, then hundreds. The man in black crossed his arms and nodded. "Always good to see a plentiful harvest. Plant the dead in the ground, and when it's time, out they come." He breathed deeply. "Appetizing."

He finally turned to the chapel itself. Its lamps burned bright. Singing floated into the night. Something about a promised land and swords into ploughshares. Nothing he hadn't heard a thousand times before. He took off his hat as he entered.

The congregation pleaded as they sang. The parson stood in the front, singing as loudly as he could.

"Ah, Mark Dies!" the Landowner called.

The singing died away.

"I welcomed you here. Gave you a new home. What will you pay me?"

The parson's face turned a terrible shade of pale. "I've never seen you before," he croaked.

"Oh, we've never met, but you know me well." The Landowner stepped forward down the aisle.

Around him, the townspeople who had come for asylum backed as far away as they could. An old man croaked a spiritual, something about a garden.

The man in black turned to look at him. "Catchy tune."

The man fell silent.

The Landowner strode forward. "Mark Dies. What will you pay me?"

Mark sighed and stepped forward, his eyes on the ground. He didn't fight. He didn't say a word. He knew how much he owed.

The rest of the people cowered as the man in black escorted his final soul of the night out into the darkness.

The train was coming.

10.

Most of the town milled around the train station. Some wept. Some shouted. Most simply stared, glassy-eyed.

A few had been transformed. Here an old couple that had been young. There a young woman that had been a man. There a boy with the face of a buzzard.

Most, though, were simply themselves. They didn't need to be changed to reveal how ugly they really were on the inside. They didn't need to show the world how evil they were. They owed the Landowner, and now it was time to pay up.

A lonesome whistle sounded.

Those who still had any ability to react turned to the west. No train had ever come to town, at least not that any of them could remember. There were no rails, after all. Still, something twinkled in the distance.

It drew closer. A black engine with vibrating pipes and pulsating veins and terrible acrid smoke puffed into the station. It pulled six cars. The windows of each dripped tears.

The people boarded. They climbed onto the cars. Some sniffed as they looked back on Scar Ridge. They remembered the joys they'd experienced. They remembered how they'd come to this terrible place.

They turned onto the cars. The seats were made of tree bark. The flickering lights burned human hair. Blood puddled on the floor.

It didn't take long for everyone to enter.

The man in black glanced around the town one last time.

"Well. I'll be back to collect taxes next year, same time." He touched the brim of his hat and boarded the train.

The engine puffed and moved into the distance.

ABOUT THE AUTHOR

Jonathon Mast lived in the Dakotas, once on a time, and he knows what it is to have the sky glare at him. He glared back, but it didn't seem to do much.

He lives in Kentucky now, with his wife and an insanity of children. His short stories have appeared in Dark Owl Publishing's *Something Wicked this Way Rides* and *A Celebration of Storytelling*, and numerous other anthologies and magazines. Dark Owl also published his first novel, *The Keeper of Tales*. He also writes middle grade science fiction and fantasy for Dawnsbrook Press. Learn more at dawnsbrook.com. You can track Jonathon down at jonathonmastauthor.com.

"A rare and refreshing level of pure pulpy fun."
~ Gregory L. Norris,
Author of the Gerry Anderson's Into Infinity novels

Written and Illustrated by

JASON J. MCCUISTON
Author of Project Notebook

VOLUME I AND VOLUME II
AVAILABLE IN PAPERBACK AND ON KINDLE

THE PHANTOM WORLD
AVAILABLE ON KINDLE FOR ONLY $1.99

THE CRIMSON STAR SAGA EPISODES
AVAILABLE ON KINDLE FOR ONLY 99 CENTS EACH

www.darkowlpublishing.com/the-last-star-warden